P9-CAE-358

– PRAISES –

"With Curtis one knows at once … he identifies with his environment, asserts his authenticity, his sense of truth, his response to his own life and to that of his kin with a gift of language at its finest and most expressive."

Jehanne B. Salinger Carlson
Monterey Herald

"What gets it all beautifully together are the pace and style Mr. Curtis brings to his story …"

Martin Levin
New York Times Book Review

"Jack lives a life as tightly connected to nature as anyone I've ever known."

Russell Chatham
Clark City Press

"Curtis brings an eloquence and wit often missing in other books of the genre."

Doris R. Meredith
Western Books in Review
Roundup

"Three fingers of Curtis in a quiet corner goes down very smoothly."

Eddy Lopez
Fresno Bee

"The author makes you feel that you are there as he shapes his characters in such a believable manner."

Don Warren
The Western Review

"Heartily recommended."

Booklist

"Jack Curtis is one of our regional best."

Russ Leadabrand
The Cambrian

"'I want to get the writing. I want to get the poetry. I want to get the humor. I want to get the music,' he said, 'I don't want to be one-dimensional, I want to be three-dimensional.'"

Jim Cole Interview
The Coast Weekly

"It's wonderful, but like all of Curtis, original enough that those of extremely conventional tastes may find it strange ... If you're not already a Curtis fan, try it."

Steve Bodio
Gray's Sporting Journal

"Jack Curtis has established himself as one of the best ... his spare style and sharp eye for character will keep his books fresh well into the coming century."

Loren Estleman

"Curtis though using a familiar form still possesses the ability to provide a new wrinkle for an old story."

Lawrence Clayton
Abiline Reporter News

"One damn fine writer!"

T. Elton Foreman
Riverside Press Enterprise

Christmas in Calico

Books by Jack Curtis

POETRY

Green Again
A Pigeon Wind
Cool of a Kansas
Arctic Circle
Water Moon of a Woman
Occupations
Poemas Reciente
Man In Place

NOVELS

The Kloochman
Banjo
Red Knife Valley
Eagles Over Big Sur
The Quick and the Dead
Hideout Canyon
The Quiet Cowboy
The Mark of Cain
Cut and Branded
Wild River Massacre
The Fight for San Bernardo
Blood to Burn
Paradise Valley
The Jury on Smoky Hill
Pepper Tree Rider
No Mercy

Christmas in Calico

An American Fable

by
Jack Curtis

PO Box 1924
Monterey, CA 93942

First Edition

Copyright 1996 Curtis Family Trust
All rights reserved.

Printed in the United States of America

All characters in this book are fictitious and any resemblance to actual persons, living or dead, is purely coincidental.

Library of Congress Catalog Card Number   *96-78047*

ISBN 0-9640537-1-3

Cover design by Don Eddy

For LaVonn

My wife's wet face is sweeter than apples
Heaped in my hands …

WATERMOON OF A WOMAN

Chapter One

"*D*ashing thro' the snow, in a one-horse open sleigh,
Oe'r the fields we go, laughing all the way..."

The lone lamp on the kitchen table cast its yellow light
like the glow of the winter sun at day's end when twilight
softens the volcanic rimrock, shades the stark poverty of
drought burned land, and mellows the bleak, boxy structures
of an unseasoned ranchstead.

"Bells on bob-tail ring, making spirits bright,
Oh what fun it is to ride and sing a sleighing song tonight!"

The golden lamp light veiled the uneven table top, obscured the cast iron cooking stove, the rough sawn boards of
the inner walls, the mismatched furnishings and the bare
plank floor.

"Jingle bells! Jingle bells! Jingle all the way!
Oh what fun it is to ride in a one-horse open sleigh!"

"Sing with me, Tommy..." she tried to encourage her
young son, bundled up on an old Morris chair near the stove.
"Dashing through the snow..."

As she sang, Rose Cameron big and bulky from her preg-
nancy, worked at a pad of folded colored paper turning and
twisting her scissors while the pale boy watched as if he'd
seen too many sleight of-hand tricks in his short lifetime.

"In a one-horse open sleigh..."

A tentative whine of unkind wind tuned the stovepipe's guy wires and in the distance coyotes on the move howled their hungry lamentations.

Hollow-eyed, the boy watched silently as his mother placed the scissors on the table and pinching either side of the folded paper between her fingers, opened up a necklace of dancing paper children, all alike, and holding hands.

"It worked," she said, smiling and shook the paper children to make them dance.

"Real nice," the boy whispered.

Around the green crown of a sweet smelling desert juniper standing in the corner, she draped the dancing figures like a lacy skirt around the compact top branches.

"Now! There's a real Christmas tree!"

"Could we put a star on top?" the boy murmured.

"Sure," his mother said, and as she returned to the lamplight, the coyotes' blood-scent cries sounded closer.

"They're hungry," the boy warned.

"They don't get their Christmas dinner here," his mother smiled, and finding a stiff piece of paper, quickly cut out a five-pointed star.

"They're right outside, mama!"

Moving to the door, Rose lifted a double barreled sawed off shotgun from the wall, snapped it open and chambered two brass cased shells loaded with buckshot.

Quickly she jerked the door open and without aiming, fired a shot to the left of the porch. The flame flaring from the short barrel illuminated two ribby coyotes transfixed before a flimsy pen. In the next instant, the pair leaped to one side and ran for the hills.

The shotgun bloomed again, hurrying the coyotes back to their natural domain.

From the pen came nervous warblings of turkeys ready for market.

As the sun failed and the wind tapped out a warning message on a loose shingle, Nellie Damker hunkered down on a stool by the placid brown cow, her forehead in the warm flank as she milked, her hands squeezing close to the udder then compressing downward to press out long jets of milk ringing against the side of the tin bucket in a quick, forceful rhythm.

When Nellie felt the bag lighten, she stripped the four tits one by one between thumb and forefinger to keep the last of the milk from caking up inside, shifted the bucket and despite her aching knees, got to her feet and stood alongside the cow in the soft twilight.

A short, powerful woman with graying hair, Nellie Damker stood listening to the shingle's tap-tap-tap, and spoke to the cow like an old friend, "Storm coming, Queenie."

The cow continued to feed on the dusty hay, unmindful of the lethal tricks of weather in the Great Basin country, and the squat, muscular woman squinted her eyes in a habitual gesture, indicating she was weighing the pros and cons of a new course of action.

I'm not going to turn you out," she decided. "Better all around if you stay inside out of the storm."

Her mind settled, Nellie Damker, wearing a rough wool sweater and a shapeless calico dress that hid her legs bowed from a lifetime of hard work and child bearing, carried the bucket outside, latched the barn door, then trudged across the yard to the old stone and log ranch house.

The heavy kitchen door was made of split pine logs thick enough to stop an arrow and most bullets, and as Nellie went on inside she wished they'd been able to put in bigger windows when they first built the place, but at that time her husband was thinking more in terms of gun ports than sunny casements.

She couldn't complain. They had survived because he'd been right.

Placing the bucket on her work table, she saw his big shape in the gloom, and said, "Why don't you light a lamp instead of settin' there worryin' yourself sick?"

"I'm not worryin' myself sick," Colonel Wayne Damker replied too quickly, his voice edged with anxiety.

Still, in a moment, he struck a phosphor with his heavy thumbnail, lifted the lamp's chimney and touched fire to the wick. Settling the glass chimney back into its wire keepers, he adjusted the wick so that the lamp didn't smoke but gave out a pure golden light that softly illuminated the big room.

Damker, a tall man with sloping shoulders, got to his feet and paced around the table restlessly, his granite-like visage partly hidden by an iron grey mustache that curled around to meet his thick sideburns.

"You'd set there all night in the dark just to save on coal oil," she said shortly, covering the milk bucket with a clean flour sack.

"Don't start ridin' me," he said, his face darkening. "This drought lasts much longer, you'll wish you'd listened to me."

"I been listenin' to you for forty years talkin' about workin' hard and savin' up so's we'd have a time later on to enjoy ourselves," she countered.

"A woman can throw away more with a spoon than a man can bring home in a wagon," Colonel Wayne Damker gave his customary sure-win reply.

"First it was the Indians," Nellie held to her train of thought, "then it was the rustlers, then it was the squatters, and now it's the drought."

"And we won every time, too," the Colonel said with pride in his voice.

"The way you been talkin', we haven't won anything," Nellie snapped at him. "Sounds like we're about to be starved off the ranch and sent to the County poor farm."

"Calico County's too poor to have a poor farm," the Colonel replied without humor.

"If you hadn't been so hard on the boys, we'd have us some help," she muttered, going to the stove and chunking in more wood.

"Made independent men out of 'em, didn't I?" the Colonel said, more belligerent now, as if she'd touched a nerve more sensitive than the others. "They're all doing well wherever they are."

"You don't see any of 'em bringin' their little ones for a visit, do you?" she nagged, a habit the Colonel usually ignored.

"None of 'em live this side of the Sierras, woman!" Damker came back at her sharply, "What are you blamin' me for?"

"Oh, I don't know," the stumpy, wizen-faced woman sighed. "I guess it's the blizzard in the air makes me hellacious."

"We been through aplenty of northers," the Colonel said. "Another one shouldn't bother you."

"Maybe its just I'm gettin' lonely out here in my old age," Nellie said. "Maybe I get tired of talkin' to my cow."

"I never said it would be easy," the Colonel said, his voice softening. "I know it's lonely for you, but I can't help it if the nearest female lives six miles over the hills."

"It's not the six miles, you know that," Nellie said, her real point coming to the surface, "it's that I've got no way to go and you'll never take me."

"By god, woman," the Colonel rumbled, "we get through this drought, I'm goin' to buy you a fancy buggy and a pair of matched carriage horses just so you can gallivant around and quit your yappin' at me!"

"I'm going to hold you to that," Nellie said, chuckling. "Don't forget."

"I'm going to have to get up before daybreak if this norther keeps building up," the Colonel said, frowning. "Me and Shorty will have to see to the cattle."

"I guess you're saying you want your supper right away," Nellie said, putting an iron pot on the stove.

"Maybe it doesn't make any difference," the Colonel said, a note of despair in his voice, "but we've got to hold on 'til we get some moisture."

"It'll come," Nellie said confidently, spooning bacon grease into the pot. "Be glad it's not neighbors shootin' neighbors."

"It gets harder and harder," he said grimly, "but there's nothing I won't do to keep this ranch going."

The sprawling adobe house stood on a slight rise above a dry stream bed protected on three sides by wooded cliffs. Its roof was made of log rafters covered by smaller straight palo de arco branches heavily plastered with adobe, which in turn was protected by a mat of reeds and grasses cut and hauled from the distant Carrlzo Sink.

It made a cool house in summer and a warm house in winter, and it was very old.

Around the house a rock wall stood high enough to keep animals out of the garden and the fruit trees, as well as the grape arbor near the back door where in the summer, hammocks hung as well as bird cages containing rosy flinches and a chattering nuthatch, and an old green parrot prowled about.

Between the house and the stream bed was a dug well topped by a rustic windlass frame for drawing water. Farther down the slope were sheds and pens made of flat rocks piled one on the other without mortar.

Passing under the gnarled and leafless grapevines, a rounded young woman wearing a quilted dress and a woolen shawl hurried to the well, attached a bucket to the rope and quickly lowered it down.

The cliffs cut off the feeble afternoon sun, creating an indirect mingling of fading light and making an illusion of comfortable gentility from what was in reality a hard-scrabble sheep ranch.

Hauling up the bucket, the woman listened to the wind's treble shriek in the cliff side junipers, looked hopefully down the trail that curved around the hill, then carried the bucket back to the house.

Inside, she spoke cheerfully into the darkened room lighted only by the flickering coals in a fireplace made of shaped soapstone, "Mucho ojo!"

From the pine vigas hung handy garlands of red chiles, braided garlic, dried chorizos, and bunches of sage, yerba

santa, yerba buena, and mormon tea that scented the room
along with the redolent mutton beria simmering in an iron
pot over the fire.

"Valgame Dios!" she said to an unseen person she knew
was sitting in a shadowed chair by the fireplace, "Abuelita,
it's going to be bad tonight."

"Asi es," came the faint and unworried response, "So
it is."

"When do we eat mama?" came a boy's voice from across
the room.

"As soon as you all have cleaned the pebbles from the
beans and your father comes home, Natine," the chunky
woman replied. "Maybe you better light some candles so you
can see which is which."

"Let me!" the boy called Natine, short for Fortunato, his
father's name, cried out ahead of the others; hurried to the
fireplace and touched a splinter of pitch pine to the fire. Going back to the table, he lighted two beeswax candles revealing all four small children at the big country table. The oldest
was the five year old boy, Natine.

"Anaberta, where is 'Nato?" the old woman by the fire
asked peevishly. "He's never home any more."

"He must try to save the sheep, little grandmother," the
rounded young woman, Anaberta, said respectfully. "The
drought makes it very hard."

"His father would have found water enough," the old
lady said, as if it were the fault of Anaberta that it hadn't
rained for three years.

"Pablito, don't drop the beans on the floor, please,"
Anaberta said to the second oldest boy, "Perhaps we will be
very glad to eat them someday."

"A la mejor cocinera se le queman los frijoles," the old woman chuckled. "Even a good cook burns the beans sometimes."

"It is time to eat bunuelas, not beans," little Pablo said, giggling. "Christmas is coming."

How lucky I am, Anaberta thought as she half filled a pottery bowl with corn flour. Even with four beautiful children and another on the way I still have less than twenty-one years and my handsome husband tiene huevos de oro.

Much as she respected her mother-in-law, she wished she had someone else to talk to. Her sisters from Sonora would visit in the coming spring and summer, and they would all have a lot of fun, but the winters kept everyone inside too much.

Sometimes, if there was a warm spell, she could go in the wagon to Calico and buy supplies, but she'd heard the storm warnings outside, and knew they were going to be house bound.

Still, she had many things to be thankful for. The old house her husband's father had built long ago, so warm and quiet, and plenty of food in the pantry, and plenty of hot burning mesquite wood in the mud room, and warm woolen clothes, and blankets…

"Mama, papa's coming!" the oldest boy called out and ran to the door.

Anaberta's husband, Fortunato Fajardo, stepped inside as if shoved by the wind, and quickly latched the door shut before more cold could enter.

"Hola! Buenos tardes!" Anaberta called out and rushed to take her husband's hat and sheepskin coat.

Tall and thin, he stooped to kiss Anaberta's cheek, then greeted his mother, and lastly went to the table and kissed each child.

"How is it out there, papa?" Little Natine asked.

"It will be a big storm," Fortunato Fajardo replied. "Let us pray it brings much snow with it."

"I don't like so much snow," Pablo said, shaking his head.

"But when the snow melts, there is much water," the father said, "and if there is much water, there is much green grass to feed the sheep and the horses."

"Where is Nacho?" his wife asked.

"Putting the sheep inside out of the weather," Fortunato said. "He'll be along in a minute."

"But there is no hay," Anaberta said, frowning.

"No," Fortunato shrugged, "we must take them out on the range again tomorrow and hunt for grass."

Without the heavy coat, Fortunato looked slim as a ramrod. Dressed in close fitting black wool shirt and trousers, he also habitually wore a mother of pearl handled Colt .44 revolver low on his hip.

Unbuckling the black gunbelt, he handed it to Anaberta who dutifully hung it on a peg near the door.

"I keep wishing you would leave this at home," she murmured. "I worry."

"Tomorrow it is yours," he said, smiling at her.

"If your father had had such a fine gun," his mother grumbled from the corner, "we would still have a grand rancho."

"I doubt if it would have made any difference, mama," Fortunato replied politely. "We didn't really own all the land, we only used it with the Paiutes' permission."

"Still, your father grazed cattle and sheep all over this country, clear to the mountains," his mother said sharply.

"You're exaggerating by about fifty miles, mama," Fortunato replied, chuckling. "Really he went from here westerly to just past the Bar D and on around north of the Circle C."

"But it all worked right for him," his mother insisted. "If there was no rain for awhile, he could move his flocks someplace else."

"He couldn't keep it all," Anaberta said in a mild tone of voice, "but we will get along fine anyway because we still have more than we need."

"I hope that is true, mi corizon," the tall, lean sheep man said softly. "I hope that gun hangs there forever."

In the sudden dusk, with the sun dropping behind the western mountains, the rider decided that night didn't descend from the heavens, but instead burgeoned up out of the earth like a huge black furry toadstool, swallowing his horse, himself, and the whole rolling country they rode.

Unthinking, the rider ignored the pull of the darkness until the stud abruptly dipped his shoulder and whirled to the right.

"Dang fool!" the rider snapped angrily, regaining his seat and jerking hard on the reins.

The black horse didn't respond, but stopped and waited for his rider to wake up and use his head.

"What the devil?" he muttered, suddenly realizing that darkness had caught him while he was dreaming of days gone by.

Dismounting, he blindly stepped forward until he felt the earth shift beneath his boots, and peering ahead he saw the cut bank that dropped steeply off into a dry wash.

"Sorry, I wasn't lookin'," he said apologetically to the horse.

Leading the way, he walked along the edge of the cut bank until he found a path angling down into the wash where the ground was level and out of the crisp breeze that seemed to arrive as suddenly as the night.

Mesquite branches, dry and brittle, made a small smokeless fire yielding enough light to show a patch of dry grass off to one side, and a sandy flat where he could lay out his buckskin bedroll.

"Won't be any snakes or gila monsters, Coalie" he murmured aloud as if the big black could understand, "Too cold and dry. We'll have to find water in the morning."

Settling down by the fire, he chewed on a tough and peppery chunk of venison jerky and listened to the ominous wail of wind overhead and thought it would have been smarter to head directly in to Calico where he could have put Coalie in a livery barn, bought himself a hot meal, and slept in a bed.

Don't much trust towns or the people in them anymore, he reproached himself. Trusted Jeff because I knew he was harmless no matter how fiddle footed his ways.

He heard the horse munching on the dry grass, his hooves thumping the soft ground, and remembered how Coalie had sensed the cut bank and turned aside, and thought he'd better not start doubtin' his horse too.

Got to find a job, he thought moodily, cattle ranch, horse ranch, Billy goat ranch, potato ranch, some little out of the way place where you don't need to fool with people, just do what the boss says and keep quiet.

There won't be any work in this droughty country. Folks ain't hirin', they're leavin', lookin' for water. Got to ride west for work. There will be water in the Truckee, water in the Carson, water in the Walker. Where there's water, there's work...

Unbuckling his gun belt, he checked the worn Colt .44 in the crisp moonlight, making sure a live cartridge would be under the hammer if and when it was needed, then tucked the revolver inside the saddle next to the sheep wool where it would stay dry and still be within easy reach.

Won't be any dew tonight, he thought, hearing the complaint of the wind rising. More like snow if it's not too dry... maybe just more damn dust...

Thinking about the cold, he unfolded his buffalo coat and laid it over the soogan.

Should have gone on into town, he thought again, a man could freeze to death out here in a sudden norther.

Spreading his big work hardened hands over the fire, he thought of the morning he'd found Jeff gone from camp, and he clamped his jaws together, trying to force his thoughts elsewhere.

Nice little fire, he told himself. Fire's like a friend if you treat it right...

Looking down into the rosy mound of coals he saw the outline of a face, saw the scrubbed fair features, the reddish yellow hair, the wide laughing eyes blue as blueberries, the cocky smile that got him into more trouble than if he'd been sour and hostile. Couldn't ask for a more cheerful sidekick except for his skylarkin' ways and his foolish trust in folks.

Gazing spellbound at the face rippling in the coals' heat, he noticed the white ash forming on the surface, and thought sadly, you're fadin' away Jeff, no matter how much wood I put on the fire, you're fadin' away...

Then, suddenly furious with himself, he cried out to the night wind, "It wasn't my fault, you knot headed idiot! I told you plenty of times! Don't lay it on me, I'm not the guilty party!"

Crawling into his bedroll, he lay his head on the saddle and haunted, closed his eyes against the accusing moon. As he drifted off to a ghost-riddled sleep he thought he heard two distant shots thumping on the wind, but they might just as well have been a falling tree or a coyote nosing out a pair of dusky grouse...

Chapter Two

*S*leet peppered Rose Cameron's lean face as she stepped carefully down from the plank porch to the bare, hard packed yard. From the abundant shape of her, she was close to term. In her arms she carried the boy bundled up in a patchwork quilt, his head high on her broad shoulder, his pale, pinched face almost lost in the folds of the comforter.

A tall country woman, made all the stronger by never-ending ranch work, she'd harnessed the team to the buckboard as soon as she'd seen the radiant daub of black and silver lifting over the western mountains and felt the bone chill knifing in on gusts of Arctic wind.

She'd packed a few clothes and the short shotgun, touched her son's feverish forehead for the hundredth time and, fighting off the sense of implacable doom moving against her, had held her good smile until the oncoming cloud undercut her hard held hopes that nature would relent, the storm turn aside and give her a little time.

Close by the ranch house a makeshift poultry pen of cedar limbs, scraps of lumber, pinyon posts, oak shakes, and half a derelict wagon bed, shook under a sharp blast of wind.

A small red eye peered out at her, blinked, and moved on. A high pitched warble of complaint came from the pen as the ungainly white turkeys slowly creaked about, sensing the force of the oncoming polar storm.

"Dimdammit, I'm doing my best!" she rebuffed the complaining flock. "I'll be back tomorrow... I'll try.... All right, I hear you!"

She glared at the ominously lowering sky again, shook her head grimly, turned away from the pen, and carried the boy to the buckboard where she'd made a secure nest of blankets and comforters on the seat.

Easing her burden down, she touched the boy's dark hair and murmured, "Hang tight, Tommy."

"I'm all right, mama—" the boy started to say, but a fit of coughing clogged his voice and wracked his thin shoulders.

Ruggedly built, with russet hair and ruddy cheeks, Rose Cameron looked strong enough to handle almost any problem on the ranch, but her worried eyes revealed a growing resignation as she gazed at the empty corrals, a barn built of rough sawn lumber, empty except for a few laying hens nesting in dark corners, the vacated two room house, the bare yard, and the iron grey clouds moving implacably closer.

"Got to do it...." She shook her head angrily, hurried back into the cabin, reappearing a moment later dragging half a sack of shelled corn.

Opening the gate to the turkey pen, she dumped the corn inside.

"Might be I should just turn you loose, but I'm betting I'll be back," she muttered to the heavy white birds clustered about the corn. "No, make it me and Tommy and whosus.... we'll all be back."

Hurrying to the buckboard, she clutched a man's sheepskin coat around her shoulders, then discovered she couldn't just spring lightly into the buckboard as she had in other times.

She had to stop, raise her left foot to the iron step, grab hold of the wagon seat with both hands, drag her heavy body aboard, then push herself erect on the seat before she could uncoil the reins from the whipstock.

On a rise off to the east of the house in a small fenced-in plot, a single headboard held against the rattling wind, and looking up that way, Rose Cameron murmured, "We'll be back, Jim."

Glancing down at the bundled up boy, she saw his tired eyes sunken in his fevered visage, set her jaw and slapped the reins.

As the team gladly moved out with the wind at their tails, she looked once more at the grim, drought ridden landscape where dust stained the first pecking sleet, while high overhead a strange wailing of new winds played like a wintry, tragic chorus. She shivered with a deep feeling of abandonment as if she were leaving a tried and true way of life, but in a moment she recovered, assuring herself that they'd return as soon as the oncoming storm passed by, and she would somehow continue to hold the Circle C Ranch.

As the buckboard cleared the gate of the ranch yard, a speck of black appeared off to the east, dust blowing away from an oncoming horse's hooves.

"What kind of a trick they tryin' to pull on us now, Tommy?" she muttered, holding the team back, her eyes hard as grey flint.

The boy, deep in his blankets, barely heard her. He didn't know why they were stopped. Mostly he wanted to sleep, to separate himself from his aching bones, yet he wanted to help too.

"Mama—" he tried.

"Don't mind my fussing," Rose said, looking down into the child's eyes, "we'll get moving soon as I settle this."

As the stranger closed, she saw he rode a black horse with heavy shoulders and bulging neck, a stud, and she wondered about that.

Few men cared to ride a stallion because they were unpredictably tricky and murderous. The more placid and dependable geldings were preferred. Mares were as irresponsible as the studs, not because they were savage and fractious, but because they were frivolous in season.

A heavy gust rocked the buckboard, reminding her of the blizzard advancing with a destructive fury over the northwest ridge like a steel scythe cutting across the high Nevada plateau.

To the west the Bar D ranch hands would be bringing in extra horses in case the cattle broke through their southern drift fence, and off to the east through the crags of the Calico hills, Fortunato Fajardo and his herders would be bringing their sheep into rock walled pens for shelter, while to the southeast, some fifteen miles, the town of Calico would be cowering before the storm like a punished dog.

The rider was big, taller than she, yet he rode with the sure steadiness of a man born to the saddle and in some way kin to the horse, matched in blood and spirit.

As he drew nearer, she saw the black untrimmed mustache shagging across a leathery, weather-lined visage and that his bulkiness was more from the buffalo robe he wore than any excessive weight he might carry. The robe was split partly in the back so that the tails covered his legs down to his boots, and the collar was turned up to meet the brim of his black Stetson that nearly hid his wind-rawed face.

Staring directly into his deep-set blue eyes, she asked flatly, "Looking for something, Mister?"

"Just headin' over toward Carson, ma'am," he said evenly.

"That's a killer storm bearing down on us." Rose gestured at the oncoming cloud. "You're too late."

"I saw the ranch house from down the trail...."

"And thought you could settle in?" she cut him off impatiently. "It's not just my neighbors, now it's come to be any stranger on the trail."

"Beggin' your pardon, ma'am, is your husband here?" he asked carefully, his honest eyes steady on hers, not as an attempt at domination, but saying in effect, no matter all our differences, we are at least equal.

"Jim Cameron is up there on the rise," Rose said, glancing over at the knoll. "That's where he's been since last May."

"I'm sorry ma'am," the rider responded sympathetically, and added, "I wouldn't mind sleeping in the barn."

Rose shook her head, "You'd freeze to death in the night. There's not a stick of firewood left. Best you ride back into Calico with me."

"I'm not much of a one for towns." the stranger said.

Rose stared at the big rawboned man, wondering for a moment if he was on the run from some great crime or other, then decided she didn't want to know. The sense of courteous virility that showed in the way he sat his horse and in his plain manner of speaking was a quality she admired, but seldom saw. Rich or poor, he was to her mind what a man should be.

"Me either" she said, breaking the tension with an easy smile. "But I don't have a choice."

Tommy elbowed his face clear of the covers and said fiercely, "We don't want you staying here. This place is ours!"

"Steady on, Tommy," Rose said softly, putting the blanket back in place.

"Maybe you could use a hired hand," the rider said without hope.

"I had a hand who could talk the hide off a cow. I thought maybe you were him." Rose said, lifting the shotgun from under the robe, then stowing it back again. "Turned out he stole our stud and likely the best mares too. After he skedaddled, what few cattle we had sprouted wings and disappeared."

"I'm not a thief, ma'am" the rider said, not saying that he liked her steady eyes, her womanly endurance, her face honest as a looking glass.

"The cupboard's about empty. Water's scarce. The hay's all gone. Only thing is my turkeys, if they don't freeze to death," she tried to explain.

"I was wishing this was a cattle ranch." His smile was ironic, mocking all the wishes that never came true.

Still trying to explain it straight, Rose said, "My husband wanted to raise blooded horses, but with the drought and some mighty strange neighbors helping themselves, there's hardly anything left except the birds."

"I like turkeys a little less'n I like sheep," the tall rider murmured, the double-edged smile grooving upwards.

"It's no joke," she came back at him strongly. "There's thirty-five of them full grown. Three of them keepers. Doesn't sound like much but they'll pay the banker his interest."

"And you're some bothered I might help myself."

"You better not!" the small boy piped up fiercely.

"Easy there, lad," the stranger said, "I'm on your side."

"I wouldn't blame you, seein' as you'd be hungry," Rose said, "but I can't afford that kind of hospitality just now."

"Place could stand some fixin' up," he said, surveying the yard, the sagging gate, the patched roof, the hodge podge turkey pen. "I could give you a hand until you're back on your feet."

"I'll say it again. Forget the Circle C. Clear enough?"

"Clear as a window pane, ma'am" he nodded "You go ahead and get that boy to the doctor. I'll just ride north and find some timber for shelter."

"There's no time. Even on that stud, you'd come up short." she said, shaking her head resignedly. "So, go ahead, make yourself at home. There's not much, but you're welcome to it."

"That's mighty kind of you, ma'am." the stranger said, "I'll keep the coyotes out of your turkey pen."

"Watch out for the neighbors too," she said bluntly, "I'm Rose Cameron. What's your name and what do you do?"

"Joel Reese, cowhand, and I'll be gone soon as the weather settles down."

"I take that as a promise, Mr. Reese. Merry Christmas." she said, and slapped the reins on the rumps of the restive horses.

The team lined out at a steady trot down the trail, going south along Calico Creek that for the most part was dry, the scanty water running underground except when it hit a solid rock basin where it would rise up to form a pool.

Tall and unbending, the man in the black robe watched the buckboard travel on south until it disappeared through a cleft in the hills, then turned the stallion toward the barn, studying the lay of the nearly lifeless ranch as he went.

After unsaddling the black inside the barn and rubbing him down with an old barley sack, Reese looked in vain for a flake of hay or a scoop of grain.

She hadn't lied, Reese thought, there wasn't anything for the stud to eat, but at least he was out of the weather.

"I'll see if I can rustle up something for you," Reese muttered to the horse and slinging his bedroll over his shoulder, leaned against the wind and sleet as he crossed to the house.

Inside was about what he expected. A bedroom, then a larger central room with a kitchen table, and an iron cook stove.

Embers still glowed in the stove, but the wood box held only a few chunks of rotten sycamore.

Somberly, he lay the bedroll by the door, then put a chunk of punky wood in the firebox to keep it going while he went outside looking for more.

Unbarring the door of a tidy root cellar dug down into the slope at the back, he found only a sack of sprouting potatoes.

"Better than locoweed," he murmured, lifting up the sack and carrying it down to the barn.

The heavy shouldered stud wasn't interested. He sniffed at the sprouted potatoes and turned away.

"You'll find them spuds mighty tasty later on," Reese muttered to the horse. "It'll be forty below before morning, best get set for it."

Over toward the creek he found a few mesquite fence posts that were too crooked to use, and carried them over to the chopping block where he cut them into stove-length chunks.

He shed the buffalo robe as he worked with the ax, and when he'd finished, the sun was obscured in a steel blue cloud, and hard sleet whipped around the cabin in a grainy spray.

The turkeys gobbled anxiously, striding about and peering through the gaps between the odd sized pickets.

Reese filled the wood box, but he knew it wouldn't last twenty-four hours. Northers like this one sometimes went on for three or four days, extinguishing all unprotected life with their crushing cold.

He searched the outer reaches of the yard for wood, but came up with only an arm load of scraps.

Grimly, he thought he might have to burn the corral rails before it was all over with. At least nature made it simple: find fuel or freeze.

Chances were that when the lady's husband was alive, he'd hauled firewood in a wagon from the eastern hills, but he hadn't been around since May.

Reese wondered why the neighbors hadn't helped.

Inside, he poked up the fire while the wind rattled a piece of tin on the roof, and the small window that looked out on the yard glazed over with frost.

Nosing through the pantry, he found a sack half full of corn meal, a jar full of black beans, and a bowl of bacon grease.

Other than salt and a can of baking powder, that was it.

From his bedroll, he took a small ditty bag partly filled with venison jerky and put it on the plank table along with the other supplies.

Wood and grub, maybe not much, but it'd have to do because the massive shoulder of the storm itself now banged against the isolate shelter.

Reese put a pot of beans to soaking, and was about to sit back comfortably in the old Morris chair and watch the snow blow by, when he recalled the blinding snow of other storms he'd survived.

Maybe it'll snow, maybe it won't, but it's best to be ready, he thought.

Buttoning up the buffalo robe again, he hurried out the door to the porch where he'd seen a saddle and discarded pieces of tack in a battered copper boiler.

The swirling sleet made it hard to see what he had to do, but pawing through the tack, he found three old lassos, and tying an end to the porch post, he walked out to the turkey pen and then crossed the yard toward the corral. About a third of the way over, the rope came taut and knotting another one to the end, he went on until it ran out. The third lasso was long enough to reach the corral fence.

Pulling the long rope taut, he tied it off on a sturdy post then followed the corral fence around to the barn door.

Taking a look inside, he saw the black had nibbled at the potatoes, and that a speckled hen was scratching at his manure on the dirt floor.

"Goin' to be cold as a witch's kiss, Coalie, but you got the fur coat for it," he said, and made his way along the fence to the rope and followed it back to the house.

Passing by the poultry pen, he noticed the turkeys had quit their nervous warbling and were hunkering down in the lee corner of the pen, clustering together to share their warmth.

"Packin' up," he muttered to himself.

Crossing over to the chopping block, he took the ax and poked the helve in between the pickets, forcing the turkeys to pull out of the pack and circle the pen again. He noticed one was a big old tom and two were large hens. Breeders, likely. After he prodded them all to their feet, he carried the ax to the front porch and left it propped alongside the door where he could always find it.

Inside he put a chunk of mesquite in the firebox and turned the damper down until the stove started to smoke, then he cracked it open just enough to draw.

"How'm I goin' to keep them turkeys from packin' up like a herd of cattle driftin' into a coulee full of snow?" he asked himself out loud.

Maybe by packin' up, they'll keep warm enough to live through the norther, he thought, and tried to remember how wild turkeys in Texas made it through the winter storms.

Seemed like they always went into the heart of the timber, then found the trees that were most protected by cut banks or high walled arroyos. They'd congregate so tightly their weight would break down the blackjack oak limbs, but they never packed up in a corner.

I daren't let those turkeys smother to death, he worried.

On the table sat a bull's-eye lantern and a regular glass chimneyed household lamp.

An opened envelope stood propped against the china sugar bowl.

He turned the envelope over in his big, rope callused fingers, then leaned over to read the name, Mrs. Rose Cameron, and the address, Circle C Ranch, Calico, Nevada.

Thinking it over, he shrugged his big shoulders and fished out the letter.

The message was brief enough.

Dear Mrs. Rose Cameron,

This is to remind you that the interest on your note to the National Calico Bank falls due January 1st. Failure to make aforesaid payment of $110.00 will regretfully force foreclosure action. I hope this doesn't catch you at a bad time.

Seasons Greetings.

Yours Truly,

Max Gotch

President

The picture began to make sense. There were no cattle nor horses anywhere to be seen. There could be some stock out on the range, but with the panic in the east and the price of beef down to due-bills, it wouldn't make much difference. Rose Cameron was counting on her turkey crop to pay the interest on her note, and if she could sell thirty-five of them, less the three parents, at five dollars a head, she'd likely be able to make it through 'til spring.

That's why she set such a store on the darned gobblers.

But surely she could find somebody to loan her a hundred and ten dollars until she could get on her feet.

Surely she had friends or neighbors that'd help.

Heck, down in Texas they'd string up a banker for worrying a widow with a child and another on the way. Just haul him off to the nearest oak tree and stretch his neck some.

He slipped the page back into the envelope and propped it against the sugar bowl again.

Three adults; two hens and a tom. They'd never make it through the blue norther in that exposed pen, but if he carried them down to the barn, they'd have a chance.

The thought crossed his mind that maybe it'd be better if he didn't interfere and just let nature take its course. She'd spoken some salty to him and told him to mind his own business, so why not just let it lay?

Because, maybe you're just a drifter, Joel Reese, he told himself, but you ain't a skunk. Besides, there was that rare wonder he felt when she looked him square in the eyes. That had to be worth something.

The cabin walls bucked against the rising wind, and he felt the frost creeping in through the wood. It was already below zero.

Hours had passed, and with the sun gone, he had no idea of what time it was. Maybe in the long run, he thought, he'd have to do the whole damn job but he hated such dirty work so much, it was better to put it off as long as possible. Still it wouldn't hurt to get the older, stronger birds out of the weather while there was plenty of time.

Lighting the storm lantern, he buttoned up the buffalo robe, put on his gloves and holding the lantern high, went out on the front porch and followed the lasso over to the door of the pen.

The eyes of a few of the turkeys flared back at the light.

Opening the door, he stooped down and found the big tom, his long pink wattle dropping down over its breast, and grabbed his legs.

Chapter Three

When Rose Cameron glanced down at her bundled up son and saw his pallid face and vague eyes, she wanted to whip up the team and race into town at a full gallop, but the rutted wagon tracks bounced the buckboard brutally even at a single trot, and she forced herself to keep the team checked to its steady pace.

She thought of the ranch and the hardship in holding it together, yet it had wrenched her spirit to have to leave it.

But why, she wondered, am I always being torn by hard choices? Leave the ranch or stay with it? Feed the turkeys or turn them out to fend for themselves? Whip up the team or give Tommy an easier ride? Give that man in black, Joel Reese, shelter or send him on the drifter's way?

Oh, Jim, she thought, maybe you put more on my shoulders than I can carry.

She thought back on the light sunny day in early spring when Jim was shoeing the horses. He'd tied on his leather apron, put his clippers, rasp and hammer in the top of his right boot, and with a set of flat nails between his lips, had worked along steadily, starting at the front hooves and then doing the back.

He'd finished the sorrel and took a minute to look around at the nearly flat land, and said to her, "Maybe it looks scrubby, but it's not, and we may be the nut in the nutcracker, but we won't be broken."

He'd meant Colonel Wayne Damker's Bar D on the west and Fortunato Fajardo's sheep ranch on the east.

"They don't have the constant water we have," he'd nodded. "nor the bottom land grass..."

"It's good land, Jim," she'd said, "and it's home."

"I'm glad you understand," he'd said gravely. "Promise me, Rose, if anything happens to me, you'll hang on to the ranch. Without land, a man isn't anything, and I want Tommy to be somebody."

"I can't think of such a sad thing," she'd replied.

"Promise me, Rose," he'd insisted.

"I'd promise you the moon for pasture, Jim, on such a fine spring day," she'd laughed, because she'd felt a cold shiver run up her backbone, and wanted to chase it away.

A little later, as he was clinching the nails on the off front hoof of the bay, a horse fly landed on the horse's withers, and the horse jerked its head around so quick it had thrown Jim off balance and a couple of the nails had raked across his forearm.

He'd settled the bay down and went ahead and finished all four hooves before washing up.

Even then he hadn't said anything until she'd seen the slashes at dinner time, and she'd torn up a flour sack to bandage it after she'd put on the carbolic acid.

Two days later Jim's arm swelled up so bad he couldn't work. He said it was just something that would heal itself, but she knew enough about blood poisoning to hurry into Calico for Doctor Snarph.

By the time she and the Doctor had gotten back to the ranch, Jim was sitting in the old Morris chair cradling his arm. His face was greasy gray with sweat and the arm was turning purple as a plum with yellow streaks running up it.

The Doctor had spread mercury salve over the arm and wrapped it in bandages.

"Change it every four hours," Doctor Snarph advised.

As she smeared on the salve and re-bandaged the arm, she'd kept on talking hopeful, telling Jim about the turkey eggs hatching and what they would name the baby boy come next December, and such things, but his face grew haggard and dark, knowing full well what he had.

The Doctor visited the next day and said it had been too late to amputate the first time he'd come out. He left some pills he thought might help.

She'd kept Tommy busy down at the barn watching the turkey poults so he wouldn't hear the groans of pain coming from the bedroom.

The next morning, when the Doctor came, Jim's face was black and his eyes dull. He was rambling on out of his head, about how they had to keep up the fences and raise up the horse herd's blood lines and such.

"Get more Morgan in 'em," he kept saying. "The Morgans never back up... Tommy top rider... the saddle... keep up the fences... Damker and Fajardo tryin' to whipsaw us... don't let 'em take it away...."

Then his vacant eyes had cleared for a second. He stared up at her and gritted through clenched jaws, "You promised me!"

Then, as if that's all he needed to tell her, his eyes closed, his body went into a convulsion that took both the Doctor and her to hold down, his black face contorted into an unforgettable rictus, and the breath rattled in his chest three times, and there was no more.

"Yes, Jim," she closed her eyes to blot out the memory and murmured aloud, "I did promise you, but what if I fail?"

Tommy coughed fitfully, the cough coming from deep in his lungs, and he struggled against his coverings.

The storm cloud covered the sky like a pewter bowl and gusting winds whipped fine, dry sleet flat across the land.

"Easy does it, Tommy," she called. "We're nearly there."

Up until Jim's accident, Tommy had been a dark haired, freckle faced, happy, healthy boy rambling around the ranch, riding double with Jim, learning to keep out of the way of an angry rooster or a fractious cow. He'd kind of fallen in love with a big chestnut broodmare in foal, and sometimes would wander over where she slept, crawl up on her swollen belly and take a nap himself.

"He thinks that mare is his mother," Jim had laughed. "I'd say that's a sign of a true horseman."

For Jim it was always horses. Let Colonel Damker raise cows, let Fortunato Fajardo raise sheep, he'd raise top riding horses on the Circle C because that's what the range was best suited for.

"The long term security is in breeding horses," Jim had insisted. "There's too many hammer-headed mustangs, and never enough quality stock. Maybe we won't get rich at it, but we'll be proud of our brand."

But after Jim died, the horses out on the range seemed to just dwindle away. She was never sure if it was that young curly haired peeler she'd hired on to handle them, or whether Colonel Damker's men or Fortunato's men had cut the fences and helped themselves, but the best of them were gone before she'd gotten herself straightened out. There was no law and no help from her ambitious neighbors.

She'd fired the young bronc peeler because she'd caught him clubbing a wild one that had throwed him.

He knew the lay of the land and where the best stock grazed.

Maybe he'd circled around later on and helped himself.

It was too late by the time she had sense enough to go out and drive what was left down into the bottom hay field. Too late. The old half Morgan stud was gone, along with his best mares.

Up ahead through the whistling sleet she saw the Calico crossing and on beyond the blurred shape of huddled gray buildings.

Off to the west the sky loomed black, even though it was only mid afternoon.

"I should have turned those turkeys out and given 'em a chance," she muttered to herself, feeling guilty. Then it occurred to her that the rider, Joel Reese, might figure out a way. He'd seen how it was with her and he looked like the sort of man who would help out all he could, even with turkeys.

"You better bring Shorty up here," Nellie said to her tall, slope shouldered husband. "He'll catch his death of cold down there in that empty bunkhouse."

"I'm glad you remembered," the Colonel said. "I was afraid if I mentioned it, you'd start screechin' at me like a bobcat in a briar patch."

"I don't screech," Nellie grumbled, a twinkle in her eye.

"I'd like to know what you call it then," the older man said with mock gruffness. "If there was ever to be a best in screechin' contest, I know who I'd bet on."

"A little vinegar is good for curing stiff necks." Nellie turned away to hide her smile.

"Only a fool argues with a skunk, a mule, or a windy woman," the Colonel said triumphantly.

"You going to let Shorty freeze or you going to go on and on like a crow with the croup?" she asked scornfully.

"I may stay down in the bunkhouse with him," the Colonel said, putting on his sheepskin coat and heading for the door. "The good book says 'It's better to dwell in the corner of the housetop than with a contentious woman in a wide house'."

"You want to talk gospel truth, I'll tell you 'Pride goeth before destruction and a haughty spirit before a fall'," she snapped back at him as he went out into the rising gale.

When he was gone, she grinned to herself, her wrinkled round face splitting into segments along the old laugh lines.

She thought he deserved a treat on this bitter night and fetched dried apples down from the cupboard, and put them to soaking.

Relying on her memory, she mixed the flour, salt, butter and warm water into a dough, divided it in two and then rolled out the bottom crust to fit her brown Rockingham pie dish.

As she worked, her thoughts inevitably moved to the past when she'd had to make an extra pie for the three boys.

Hungry as baby birds, they were always pestering her for more pie. Wayne Junior, he liked Kentucky pie if she had any pecans, and Bobby, he went for dried apricot pie like it was better'n taffy, and Rodney always wanted Fudge Cream pie. Their daddy, though, he always chose dried apple, maybe because when he was a little boy, that's what his mother baked for him.

Hard to believe, so hard he looked most of the time now, he'd ever been a little boy.

Wasn't his fault exactly except he chose to raise cattle when he could just as well have chose steam boating or being a merchant or carrying the mail.

He chose it because he knew cattle from his folks' farm in Tennessee and he didn't know much else, and he was good at it just like he was good at anything he tried.

Went to war and ended up a Colonel under General Forest. Learned to get there the firstest with the mostest, and fight to win, learned to give orders and make sure they were carried out. That's how he drove off the boys.

He couldn't come back to become just a human being. When he wanted something done, he ordered the little ones around like they were dumb recruits, she thought sadly. Was no way to change him by then. The more I tried to protect them, the harder he worked them. No answer to it. They didn't suffer, but soon as they grew up to be bigger and stronger than him, they rode off on their own. Rodney left when he was sixteen. No more Fudge Cream pie, no more dried apricot pie, no more Kentucky pie.

Just dried apple pie after that.

Still and all they were good little boys, she sighed. Someday when the work's all done, we can go over the mountains and visit each one of 'em for a little while and tease their own little kids with stories of their pranks.

Better go some Christmas time when there's nothing much to do around here except sit by the fire, and we could have Christmas with the whole caboodle in California, and I'd bake four different kinds of pie, and show their wives how to do it.

Likely though they wouldn't want to learn. They'd rather do it their own ways without an old lady sticking her nose in.

She pressed a soaked dried apple between her thumb and forefinger and decided it was about ready. After measuring out the sugar in her cupped hand, and pinches of cinnamon and nutmeg between her fingers into a bowl, she mixed in the apples, eggs, cream and butter until the filling smelled good enough to eat just as it was.

Pouring the mixture into the pie dish, she covered it with another crust rolled out from the leftover dough, then pinched the edges together using her thumb and first two fingers until the edges were neatly scalloped all around.

As a final touch, she used a small knife to cut a Capital N in the center and added three smaller individual cuts on either side. It was her special mark.

Before she married, she'd taken pies to church socials in Frankfort and everyone knew who had baked each pie by that centered decoration, like it was her brand.

But out here on the Bar D it was too far to go to a social in Calico. Never was time, either.

Nobody knows my mark, she thought. Nobody knows I'm a good baker and no one cares. Hardly anybody but Wayne even knows I'm alive....

What kind of a life is that? No wonder I'm thinking nonsense all the time. Be talkin' to myself soon. And answerin'.

There must be others like me scattered around this country. Women that never see a neighbor, never go to the socials. Just get to town once a month for supplies.

You go to the Mercantile and there's a lady with her list, buying things and by the time she's finished, you learn she's your next door neighbor—only her house is six miles over the hills.

That Mrs. Cameron is in the same boat as me, only she started a long time after I started out here. No reason why we couldn't be friends even if she's young. Somebody said she lost her husband last spring, but I didn't even hear about it until the middle of the summer... too late to take a covered dish like we used to in Frankfort.

We could talk about raisin' kids and share recipes and quilt patterns and maybe Wayne could help her for awhile until she finds another man....

We been living next door to each other for close to seven years and never visited except in the Mercantile. That's a damn scandal.

The door slamming open startled her. Turning she saw Wayne and the small puncher named Shorty, plunge through the doorway as if slammed in by the rising wind.

As Shorty closed the door, she looked over at her husband and demanded sharply, "Have you ever thought we ought to be helpin' out Rose Cameron?"

"Now whatever put that idea in your head so sudden?" the Colonel came back at her.

"Well, have you?"

"No, Nellie," the Colonel replied. "You got it backwards."

Ignacio, the herder, preferred to sleep in his own cabin near the lambing pen but on this ice-cracking night, he made up a pallet on the floor in the corner of the big house.

"Only for tonight," he said apologetically to Anaberta as they sat down at the table for supper.

"Who knows what tomorrow will bring," she replied, filling bowls with the rich, aromatic beria.

The grandmother, tall and thin as a desert tree, moved from her secluded chair and came to help Anaberta with the little ones while Fortunato brought in more wood for the fire.

The candlelight had a soothing effect on the children and the rich stew along with hot corn tortillas engaged even Pablito, who was usually the most restless and demanding.

When Fortunato came to the head of the table, he saw his mother was feeding Guadalupe, the smallest girl, and Ignacio was helping out with Carlos the next oldest brother, and he sighed contentedly.

"Let the wind blow," he said, not needing to add that he was pleased with his family, his weather-tight house, the food on the table. "And bless this house."

With so many children, food was of course spilled, voices cried out, and Anaberta was kept busy mopping up, but never was a hateful word said in anger.

Dropping her spoon, little Guadalupe stared down at the floor and cried out in consternation, "Uh-oh!"

Pablito looked up from his bowl, grinned and mocked her, "Uh-oh!"

Natine reached down and retrieved the spoon, adding his voice, "Uh-oh!", and in a minute all the youngsters were staring wide-eyed at their spoons and making a chaotic chorus: "Uh-oh!"

"Eat your supper," Anaberta pretended to scold them, but they continued with their new game: "Uh-oh!" as the wind challenged the house and the chill of the polar night slowly drew the heat from the thick adobe walls.

"Payasos!" Fortunato said with a smile. "You're all clowns. All we need now is for a big polar bear to come down the chimney."

Thinking of a polar bear coming down the chimney kept the children occupied through the rest of the supper, Natine saying he'd be ready with the iron poker and Pablito arguing that the bear wouldn't come down the chimney because he'd burn his tail off, while the next in line, Carlos insisted he wanted the bearskin for his bed, even as little Guadalupe still stared at her spoon and tried to keep her game going, "Uh-oh!"

"A la cama ! Off to bed!" Anaberta announced, and managed to herd the four children into the bedroom where they would sleep together in one bed, and the grandmother would sleep on a cot close by. Perhaps in another year, Natine would sleep in his own bed, Anaberta thought as she tucked them in, and another would take his place. So it would go.

Coming back to the big room, she saw that Ignacio had crawled into his makeshift bedroll without undressing, and that Josefina, her mother-in-law, had finished cleaning off the table.

"Will the sheep be all right?" the old lady asked Fortunato.

"We can do nothing more for them," Fortunato shrugged. "They are out of the wind, but I wish they were stronger."

"They must last till spring," his mother said firmly as if Fortunato should see to it.

"Then pray for sunshine, mother," Fortunato said, "and pray for rain, too."

"We are so lucky to have a warm house in this weather," Anaberta said, trying to ease the worry from her husband's eyes. "Many people will be having a hard time, but we are fine."

"I'm not satisfied," the old woman grumbled. "I'm worried that we'll lose the flock."

"Ni modo," Fortunato said, "Everywhere tonight people are worrying about their animals but once you have done everything you can do, there is nothing to worry about."

"If they are going to freeze you should bring the weakest ones in here," his mother said.

"It is not the freezing so much as the shortage of feed," Fortunato said. "If they were all fat as butter, the cold would be nothing to them."

"Your father would buy hay then," the old lady said gloomily.

"Hay is so expensive now, I couldn't trade the whole flock for a wagon load," Fortunato said, shaking his head. "It is this way all over from the Sierras clear to Reese River and maybe farther."

"Think of all the ranches like ours trying to live through this storm," Anaberta said.

"There are not so many left," Fortunato said. "Only the strongest have lasted this long."

"It is odd," Anaberta said thoughtfully, "we don't know any of them."

"We know the Bar D and the Circle C," Fortunato said. "We three are the only ones left in the Calico Basin."

"But I don't know them," Anaberta said, concerned. "Sometimes I see ranch women in town, but I don't even know their names."

"You are not supposed to know them," old Josefina said dully. "They are cattle people, and gringos besides."

"But we are neighbors," Anaberta said.

"I know the old Colonel and his wife," Fortunato said. "They have only one man left to help them now."

"Have they no family?" Anaberta asked.

"All gone. The Colonel still thinks he's an Army officer. It's a wonder someone hasn't put him down."

"This 'put him down'...?" Anaberta frowned.

"Shoot him dead," Fortunato said shortly. "If he ever tries to top dog me, I will see to it."

"No, esposo mio," Anaberta said quickly. "that is not the right way."

"He treats everyone, even his own family, like dogs, but he will not treat me like a dog," Fortunato said.

"Stay away from him then," Anaberta pleaded. "Don't give him a chance."

"I don't change my ways to suit his ways," Fortunato said seriously. "You wouldn't want a coward for a husband, would you?"

"First I want you alive," Anaberta said, "the rest is foolishness."

"The rest is my business, woman," Fortunato said plainly. "There's nothing more to say."

Anaberta heeded the firmness in her husband's voice and changed the subject. "What about the poor widow over at the Circle C?"

"She cannot stay there much longer," Fortunato said. "She's just wearing herself out, working like a man for nothing."

"She wouldn't do it for nothing," Anaberta said. "She must have some reason."

"No one likes to leave their home, no matter how miserable it can be," old Josefina said wisely. "It's too hard to think about starting over again."

"She has a little boy, doesn't she?" Anaberta asked.

"And one on the way, I heard," Fortunato nodded.

"And to think I don't even know her," Anaberta said, "our closest neighbor."

"There's never time for socializing out here," Josefina said. "We are always alone."

"Could we go see her Nato? Take her a little Christmas gift. Maybe her boy could come over and play with Natine."

"She is not like us," Josefina said, objecting.

"Como no?" Anaberta asked. "We're all working so hard to get through the drought, trying to raise up our children, trying to make something worthwhile of our lives...."

"That is all true enough," Fortunato said, "but maybe there are too many people in this basin. Maybe it won't support even three families."

"What are you saying?" Anaberta asked, frowning.

"I'm saying, maybe it would be better for everyone if the widow moved out," he replied.

Chapter Four

*P*iles of manure and discarded trash littered both sides of the street. Most of the buildings were quick made of green lumber, and whatever paint daubed on their fronts had been worn away by sun and wind, but the First National Bank of Calico on the corner was solidly built of brick and boasted a varnished oak paneled door.

The Calico Queen Saloon across the street had rooms upstairs reserved for homeless young women down on their luck.

The Mercantile on the opposite corner, a broad, squat building, was packed with all manner of merchandise from boots to brandy, guns to groceries. On the fourth corner of the only intersection, stood the Plaza Hotel, another square built, two story edifice boasting eight rooms for rent as well as the living quarters of the owners, Elijah Masson and his wife, Ophelia.

The rest of the haphazard buildings along the two block street held a harness maker, a butcher, Doctor Snarph's office, a livery stable, barbershop, funeral and furniture parlor, a wheelwright, blacksmith, feed, hay and fuel yard, and the marshal's office in front of the jail.

Clustered behind these commercial buildings were the simple houses of clerks and working people, while on the rise at the west end of town, stood the banker's two story, white painted house with its broad veranda, and next to that another two story residence belonging to Doctor Snarph. Be-

tween the big house and the livery barn, set off to one side
was the Calico Foursquare Temple near the foot of Boot Hill,
a brushy, unfenced knob littered with fallen markers and
grazed by wild burros.

Concerned only with Tommy's stubborn fever, Rose
drove directly to Doctor Snarph's office, halted the team,
stepped down heavily, then lifted Tommy in her arms and
forged her way through the needling wind.

Kicking the door shut, she found herself in a small, warm
room with flowered paper on the walls, four oak chairs and a
small desk.

Doctor Snarph rose from the desk, his eyes quick to recognize her and Tommy, his thin lips almost buried in a
trimmed black beard and mustache.

"Mrs. Cameron," he said, not coldly, but not with any
warmth either.

"Tommy's not well," Rose said, moving bulkily toward
the desk.

"Bring him on in," the doctor said.

He opened the door to another room and she carried
Tommy over to an examining table covered by a varicolored
tapestry material and laid him down.

Pulling the patchwork quilt away from the thin body,
she took a deep breath, leaned over and kissed the boy's pale
forehead.

"You shouldn't be lifting or overexerting in your condition," the doctor said reprovingly.

"I'm all right, Doc," she looked down at the small man,
"Tommy's the one needs attention."

The Doctor held Tommy's tongue down with a spoon and Tommy said, "ah", while the physician peered into his mouth.

He listened to the boy's chest with a stethoscope, removed the tubes from his ears and said, "Fluid in the lungs."

"He's got a fever, Doc," Rose said.

"Yes, yes, you don't need to tell me," the black bearded doctor came back at her sharply, and putting his soft, white hand on the boy's forehead, nodded.

"Well, what do you think?" Rose asked anxiously.

"It's just the croup. He needs to stay warm and get plenty of bed rest. He'll need some medicine too if there's any money."

"I know I haven't paid all of Jim's bill yet...," Rose said apologetically, "and with the drought and all...."

"I have expenses like everyone else," he said, shrugging.

"Sure, Doc, I didn't know you were in need," Rose said, her temper on the rise.

"We all must pay our bills," Doc Snarph said, his gaze shifting away as he added, "Get him a bottle of St. Jacob's Catarrh Balm for his throat and Santee's Croup Cure for his chest. A bottle of Ayer's Cherry Pectoral wouldn't hurt either. Try that for a week and if he isn't better, bring him back in."

Scribbling these names on a note pad, he gave her the slip of paper, then in a clearer hand, he wrote again.

"Your bill," he said, making an artificial smile.

She glanced down at the slip of paper, sucked in her breath, and let it out slowly before she spoke. "Five dollars for five minutes? Don't worry, doctor, I'll pay it as soon as I can."

"Keep him out of the cold," Doctor Snarph said, as Rose carried the boy out the door. "We don't want him to catch pneumonia."

When she put the boy back in the buckboard, Tommy looked up at her and said, "Don't pay him, mama."

"Hush now, Thomas Cameron," she said. "We always pay."

Once again heaving her heaviness up into the driver's seat, she clucked to the team and guided them to the far end of the street where a corral and barn bore a crudely lettered sign: Morrison's Livery Stable.

The two wide doors were closed, and bracing herself against the icy wind, she climbed down and pounded on the wooden portal.

In a moment the door opened a crack and she saw a thin, pale face with narrow, ratty eyes staring out at her.

She smelled hay, horses, and alcohol.

"Will you put up my team, Mr. Morrison?" she asked quickly.

"Two horses is four bits a day," the hatchet faced Elroy Morrison answered. "Cash in advance."

"Seems high, but I can't just leave them out in this storm." Rose dug into her knitted reticule for her coin purse. Finding two quarters, she laid them in the grimy, upturned hand, and Morrison pushed open the double doors, then helped Rose unhitch the team and lead them inside. His right leg, stiff at the knee, made him bob up and down like a rocking horse as he moved about.

Rose, holding Tommy in her arms, looked over the stable, empty except for her own two horses, and asked, "I don't suppose we could camp up in the loft until the weather breaks?"

"That'd be another four bits," Morrison said, his eyes on the horse dung at his feet.

"Maybe we'll try the hotel," Rose said, turning away.

"Mighty expensive. Heard you was down to raisin' turkeys," Elroy Morrison said, frowning.

"It's honest."

"Ain't nobody in town got work," he said, mournfully. "Price of cattle and sheep is down so far, this town'll never come back."

Rose almost said that she didn't think the town had ever gone anywhere yet, but instead she said, "It's time we all started pulling together."

"They'll be ice-skating down in the hot place when that happens," Morrison said shaking his head.

"I can walk, mama," Tommy said as Rose carried him out into the driving wind.

"It's just a ways up to the hotel," she said, trying to hide her shortness of breath by talking. "We'll just hole up there for a couple of days and get you fixed up good as new."

"I wish we had Dad".

"Sure now, we both do, but we've got to think of us and the ranch now. Come spring, things'll look a lot better."

She knew in her heart it would take a miracle for things to look any better because there would be no calf crop and mighty few colts.

Crossing the street she saw a large grey rat staring at her from under the boardwalk. She slipped in the wet manure and as she struggled to right herself, Tommy lapsed into a heavy coughing spell and fought for breath, driving an awful dread into her heart.

"Steady on there, son," she said, gaining the boardwalk at the next corner where the windswept Mercantile stood.

Remembering the medicine the doctor had recommended, she climbed the two steps to the entry way, and stepped inside where the warmth of the big cast iron stove made her feel like the world wasn't so bad after all.

Sitting in oak chairs next to the stove were George Veiten, the owner, and a toothless old man with a white beard staring at a checkerboard.

Veiten heaved his big apron wrapped belly reluctantly up from the chair and nodded to Rose. His pleated, pink jowls bobbled as he spoke with a German accent, "Afternoon, Mrs. Cameron. Bad day to be away from the ranch, ain't it?"

"I had to come in for supplies, Mr. Veiten," Rose said, sitting Tommy on the counter, and straightening her coat over her own bulging abdomen.

"Supplies?"

"Mainly some medicine. Tommy's got the croup," Rose said, handing over the slip of paper.

"St. Jacob's Catarrh, Ayer's Cherry pectoral. You know you been running a bill, Mrs. Cameron...."

"Yes, but I always pay," Rose said.

"But how?" he asked softly. "You said you'd sell Christmas turkeys, but you know what you'll find when this storm blows over."

"I left them plenty of feed, Mr. Veiten. They can tough out a little blizzard." She was saying words she didn't trust anymore. It was a simple truth that none of that flock, even the old ones, could survive a below zero blizzard.

"You got a note at the bank like everybody else in Calico County. We got to pay the interest. Takes money."

Veiten shook his head and fumbled through a drawer behind the counter for a small bottle labeled 'Santee's Croup Cure'.

Wrapping the bottle in a squill of paper, he took down a ledger and finding the Circle C account, wrote the purchase down, along with the date.

Closing the book, he said, "That's a dollar more on your bill, Mrs. Cameron. The total now is thirty-six dollars and twenty-seven cents. If it ain't paid by January first, I'm goin' to have to give it to the judge."

"Whatever would a judge do that I can't do myself?" Rose asked, frowning.

Outside, she carried Tommy up the street toward the Plaza Hotel.

"These folks are all mixed up about money, Tommy," she said to the bundled up boy on her shoulder.

"But it's the way it is," Tommy answered weakly.

"It doesn't take money to clean up this dirty street," she said strongly. "It just takes folks with shovels who want to live in a clean place."

With that she turned into the hotel entry way and opened a door with a large pane of etched glass in the upper panel.

The small counter inside, backed up by wooden pigeon holes, was deserted. Sitting Tommy on the counter, she waited for a clerk. An eight day clock ticked off the seconds until she saw the nickel plated bell at the end of the counter.

Punching the bell, she smiled at Tommy, and said, "Nice and warm in here."

Before he could reply, a woman as tall as Rose and nearly the same shape, came out of a rear door. Her hair was done up in a tight bun on top of her head.

"Yes?"

"We'd like a room until the storm breaks, Mrs. Masson."

"It's a dollar a night for the two of you. In advance."

"I'll be glad to pay later," Rose said, "I've got to get Tommy out of the weather."

"My husband is dead set against giving credit," the big woman shook her head.

"Maybe I could help out some," Rose offered.

"If you ask me, Mrs. Cameron," Ophelia Masson said, "you ought to help yourself out first by finding a good man."

"I've never seen a man as good as my Jim," Rose said, holding back her anger, "and I just doubt if I ever will."

"Best be practical," Ophelia Masson went on heedlessly.

"I didn't marry Jim because it was practical," Rose said.

"It's your business," Ophelia Masson shrugged, "but you're not getting any younger,"

"But maybe I'm getting smarter," Rose said stubbornly.

Ophelia Masson looked down at her lodger's registry, shook her head, and said, "Sorry, Mrs. Cameron, better try down at the church. Likely the preacher can figure out something for you."

As Rose awkwardly bundled up the boy and turned to leave, Ophelia Masson paused a long moment to savor her power, reconsidered and said, "Wait—"

So hurt by Mrs. Masson's coldhearted attack on her feelings for Jim and wanting no more of it, Rose pushed on out the door without replying.

Mrs. Masson pinched her pudgy lips together and stared at the door, disappointed not only in Rose, but in herself for cutting off her nose to spite her face.

She'd wanted to be friends, to share her feelings, and give her experienced advice, but Rose Cameron only wanted a room.

She'd wanted to say that it was just as lonely for an upright, outspoken woman in the little town as it was for a woman stuck out on a remote ranch with only the wind for company.

She'd wanted to talk about how she decided to marry Elijah even if he was twice her age instead of some fool frolicking cowboy, but there hadn't been a chance. Just a wooden face and she was gone without even saying Merry Christmas or good-bye.

Should have let her have the room first and then talked, she thought. Naturally she's got a lot on her mind besides a dead husband. Sick boy. Baby ready to pop.

Pushed too hard too soon... people are always saying I'm too nosy, too pushy, got a vinegar tongue hinged in the middle, but if I don't speak out, who will ever know what I'm thinking?

'Course, being older, I've got the right to speak out, she thought. Just as it's the obligation of younger women to listen and learn.

Besides, I've always lived in town and that helps a person to learn what makes the world go around, and even if I've never had any children, that doesn't mean I haven't seen enough of them idling their lives away climbing trees and playing silly games.

Her wool gathering was interrupted by a tall, hump-shouldered man with grey, bushy hair and a hangdog look on his long, lumpy face coming in the side door. Looking around the ante room, he said carefully, "I thought I heard somebody out here...."

"It was Mrs. Cameron from out in the valley," Ophelia said sharply. "She wanted a room on credit."

Looking at the floor, Elijah murmured, "It's awful cold out."

"Well, she should have remembered to bring a little money along," Ophelia said, glaring at her whipped down husband.

"I heard she was about to lose the ranch—" he stammered.

"Well, she could've said so," Ophelia said, her tone softening. "How am I supposed to know anything if nobody will talk to me?"

Elijah Masson struggled to reply, but fear was the stronger and he clamped his mouth shut before he got himself in more trouble.

"What is it?" she demanded. "Are you still trying to say I drive people away? Are you trying to say people don't even want to talk to me? If that's what you're saying, you can just run this hotel all by yourself, and I'll sit in my parlor and tat doilies!"

"I didn't say nothing," he strangled out, moving back toward the door.

"Maybe you're right, Elijah," the big woman said, suddenly morose and downcast. "Maybe if I had a baby, I could face up to people with a smile. The way it is now, I keep thinkin' they're talking behind my back, saying I'm barren and no good for nothin'. Likely the most practical thing for me to do would be to find a rope and a rafter and get it over with."

Chapter Five

*L*ighting the lamp, Joel Reese felt the house shudder under the wind's great hammer, and he went to the window meaning to look out into the yard, but a thick coating of frost, not only on the outside of the glass, but inside as well, obscured his view. Scraping at the layer of ice with his blunt thumbnail, he understood that the room was slightly warmer than the outside, but it was still freezing. The stove made the difference between life and death, so long as there was wood to burn.

Wearing his buffalo robe, he hunched over the stove, rubbing his hands and soaking in the warmth. Hefting a piece of stovewood he considered how best to ration out the little fuel that remained. It was an equation that couldn't be resolved because the wood box was nearly empty and the storm just beginning.

The cabin quaked as a heavy gust of wind smacked against the wall, and its howling sounded like a chorus of demented men crying for help.

For a moment Joel thought he recognized a voice and, puzzled, he went to the door, opened it a crack, and peered through the knife-edged wind into the darkness.

"Who's out there?" he yelled. "Jeff! Jeff, that you?"

Breaking off, he slammed the door, muttering, "Can't be you... you been dead six months... danged ghost... leave me be!"

The wind raved on, and the cries he heard were too garbled to comprehend or even be sure they were really words, but worried that a stranger might be lost in the storm, Joel lighted the bull's-eye lantern and went out into the swirling gale.

"Anybody out there?" he yelled, swinging the light against the opaque scrim of flying sleet.

He tried to listen, but there was nothing but the wind's high-pitched warnings and the sleepy warbling of the turkeys.

Moving around to their pen, he shone the light inside and saw the white feathered mass tightly clustered together in the far corner, grainy sleet tumbling in on them.

"Good thing I fetched out the keepers," he muttered, unlatching the gate. Going into the pen he poked at the mass of immobile turkeys with his boot and shook his head. "Well, you're close but you're still not as dead as old Jeff."

Deep down he'd known all along what he had to do, but he still resisted the hateful job, needing time to set himself by talking it over as loners do.

"Mrs. Cameron, I can't mother all your dumb turkeys.... And, lady you sure don't give a hoot whether I freeze to death or beller like a bent Billy goat... and nobody else does either. Well I ain't a loner by chance! You talked down to me like... like I wasn't nothin' but a fiddle-footed saddle tramp...."

Suddenly he realized that he was describing himself just as he was, that Rose Cameron hadn't talked down to him, she'd talked straight, told the truth, and met his eyes with hers, fair and square. He made a faint smile. "Well, dear lady, let me tell you, most expert saddle tramps don't go out of their way doin' favors!...."

"And besides, I hate chickens and ducks... crows and pigeons. I hate noisy guinea hens and geese and canaries—but most of all I hate dumb turkeys...."

Suddenly Joel seized the door of the pen and ripped it free of its rawhide hinges, then smashed it into stove length pieces, and piled the wood on the porch.

Returning to the pen, he searched through the passive turkeys and pulled a pair, more dead than alive, from the bottom of the pile

Hauling the unprotesting birds to the chopping block, he quickly axed their heads off and held them high off the ground so that they bled well.

Later, lifting a turkey from the steaming copper boiler, Joel let the hot water drain, then grabbed at the plastered down feathers, throwing them by the handfuls into a bucket on the floor.

"Prime stock...." he muttered disgustedly.

When he had the carcass picked clean and singed, he used his Bowie knife to cut off the lower legs and neck, removed the corn filled crop, then slitting open the rear he inserted his hand into the warm, slick cavity and carefully pulled out the guts. Saving the liver, heart and gizzard, he dumped the stinking viscera into the bucket, put the giblets back inside, wiped the turkey dry, wrapped it in a flour sack, and added it to the others packed in a wooden crate.

A feather stuck to his ear, another on his forehead, another in his nose, and he pawed at them with greasy fingers, muttering, "Hang down your head and cry, old buckaroo."

Dunking another decapitated bird into the hot water, bobbing it up and down gently, he grumbled, "You been a lot of places and done a lot of things, but I never thought you'd be cuddling up to a bunch of dead turkeys...."

Hauling the bird clear of the water and letting it drain, he added, "Ma'd be right proud of you, drifter... you keep on progressing this way, you'll be ready for matrimony...."

The hours passed by in a seemingly endless repetition of scalding, picking, butchering, dressing and packing the birds into clean flour sacks.

When he was done, there were five wooden crates filled with finished turkeys on the floor.

Each crate weighed over a hundred pounds and after he hauled them out to the subzero root cellar, he barred the cellar door and gave a great sigh of relief.

"I reckon the next downhill step is either swampin' out saloons or sellin' sewing machines...." he said, shaking his head.

Back inside, he jammed more pieces of the salvaged pen into the firebox, swept the floor with a bobtailed broom, then wearily looked around the cold room for any more vagrant feathers.

"Ain't you goin' to scrub the floor too, Miz Reese?" he mocked himself and settled down in the reclining Morris chair.

With his eyes fixed on the blue enamel coffee pot on the stove, he dozed off and saw a similar pot sitting on a rock by a small campfire, where a slim man with reddish yellow hair held a willow switch braided with thick bacon over the fire. He did not see himself hunkered on his heels close by, watching the fire, as Jeff grinned and said, "This is the tail end of the sowbelly, Joel. We're goin' to have to find work or start slimmin' down."

"I been hopin' we could get out of the cattle business and into the horse business."

"Not on thirty a month." Jeff shook his head.

"Still, they say over in Nevada there's good mustangs runnin' loose and fair land for the taking."

"We've got to keep punchin' cows just to pad our bellies unless you want to take a chance...."

"You still thinkin' about that damn bank back yonder?"

"You saw it," Jeff nodded. "You heard them simple souls talkin' about how easy it would be."

"You're thinkin' dead wrong. Every one of them dudes has a weapon and they looked starved down for excitement."

"Three years of war we never earned a peck of peanuts," Jeff said, shrugging, "and how long we been nursemaidin' somebody else's cows? Six years, seven? Pard, we ain't even seen the elephant yet."

"If we can make it over to Nevada, maybe things'll change."

"I took a long look at that bank this mornin'," Jeff said, grinning. "Just like the folks said, all it lacked was a sign sayin' 'Help Yourself'."

"We're goin' on west and let that bank keep on doing what banks do."

"Sure you don't want to hold my horse while I make a polite withdrawal?" Jeff murmured.

"Listen you idiot, you want me to hog-tie you?"

The slim drifter pulled off his right boot and lifted it high. A thin stream of sand fell from the half torn off sole.

"I reckon we can eat my boots for breakfast," Jeff chuckled. "They're sure no good for anything else."

"I'll have mine fried," he said, laying his head on the saddle and looking up at the stars.

In the morning, he groaned at the ache in his back, scrubbed at his eyes with his fists and then stared at the vacant place across from the dead fire.

"Jeff!"

Riding the stud back down the back trail, he heard the sudden cacophony of gunfire. Shotguns, muskets, buffalo guns, blunderbusses, repeating rifles, six guns.

In the distance he could make out a white steeple.

"Sounded like Saturday night in Abilene...." he muttered to the horse.

In town he halted the black near the crowd of elated townspeople and spoke to a man in a greasy white apron waving a goose gun.

"You folks havin' a turkey shoot?"

"I hit him dead center!"

"You want to view the body, what's left of him is over at the emporium having his picture took," a big man with a small derringer in his hand hollered.

"I reckon I'll pass this time. What was he after?"

"The bank! Danged fool had his gun out, but when the Marshal come at him, he couldn't shoot. Never fired a shot."

Suddenly Joel's head twisted and banged against the chair as he yelled, "Jeff, you want me to hog-tie you!"

Awake now, he wearily got to his feet and muttered, "Oh, Jeff, you danged idiot...."

Chapter Six

*T*he church, hardly more than a wooden box with a cross nailed to the peak of the roof, had a more grandiose sign over the door: Four Square Temple.

In the gloom and biting sleet, Rose Cameron slowly approached the door. By now, from weariness, she had shifted Tommy over to her left shoulder.

The icy china knob turned in her hand and she pushed the door open, looked in, felt the bitter wind cutting into her back and bumbled on inside.

Crude benches lined either side of an aisle that led down to a plain altar covered by a white sheet.

Back of the altar, on the wall, hung another cross, this one painted white and below it a frosty window.

"So cold...." Tommy murmured.

A flat topped stove stood off by the left wall but there was no fire.

"At least we're out of the wind." Rose replied.

As she sank down on one of the benches, the dark figure of a man came out of a door on the other side of the altar.

"Who is it?" the man called.

Rose stood again and went down the aisle.

"It's me, Rose Cameron," she said approaching the tall man with the bald head and vague, unfocused eyes.

"Indeed, I'm pleased to meet you, Mrs. Cameron, or have we met before?" the preacher said, rubbing his high forehead with the back of his hand. "I'm Reverend Chamberlain, pastor here, sometimes I'm forgetful... can I help you?"

"Plain and simple, my boy's sick, Reverend," she said, "and I haven't enough money to rent a room."

"That is indeed a problem.... I hear it's because of the money panic back east—the Morgans, or is it the Vanderbilts... whatever...?" Reverend Chamberlain chattered in a high pitched voice, his long features fixed in benign waxy commiseration. "Wasn't it your husband who died a few months ago? We rather expected you would ask us to say a few words at his funeral."

His words hung in the air as a reproach, as a questioning of her loyalty to his faith.

"I couldn't get over the hurt," Rose said. "It was done private."

"Of course, your friends and neighbors were there for solace," the Pastor smiled and dithered on, "that's the wonderful thing about country living, the people's moral strength... I was born and raised in Boston... matriculated from the Seminary.... Did you want the boy baptized? I don't blame you, he looks awful."

"I'd rather wait until he's old enough to make up his own mind," Rose said.

"Suppose he's struck down! Suppose we all stand at Armageddon? Suppose the devil has bewitched him?" the Reverend asked, cocking his head to one side as if judging his own oratory. "He will be cast immediately into hell. See how his face is flushed!"

"I'm not so sure God's that mean," Rose said tactfully.

The Reverend moved to the font, rapped his knuckles on the ice, and shook his head.

"Of course... no one can stay here. It's already freezing and it'll get worse. Some sects believe the world will end in fire, but from my studies, I'm of the opinion it will be quite the opposite. Death comes on a pale horse as it were, and this may very well be the fateful time."

"We could build a fire," Rose said. "There's plenty of wood."

"Wood? Man that is born of woman is of few days, and full of trouble.... think about that Mrs. Cameron, not mere wood the aldermen cut for their comfort, but of eternity and salvation...." the Reverend said, smiling sympathetically. "If we live through the night, if the end has not come, I hope you'll join our fellowship—"

"Merry Christmas, Reverend," Rose said, turning to go back up the aisle.

"Mrs. Cameron," the Reverend said, worriedly, "you might possibly find a cheap room over in shack town.... but be careful, those people will cut your throat just to steal your shoes. These are godless times, but vengeance is mine, sayeth the Lord."

"I'll speak to the banker first," Rose said stubbornly. "He's always been friendly."

She went out the door into the luminous twilight and made her way back toward the center of town with no idea of where to go to, what to do.

She saw lamplight in the bank's window as well as brighter lights in the Calico Queen Saloon across the street.

She looked from one to the other, and felt the cold twist in her bones.

Crossing to the bank, she hurried up the steps and found the door locked.

Someone was in there where it was warm and cozy, she thought and rapped on the oak paneled door with chapped blue knuckles.

She heard the footsteps, and the door opened, revealing plump and rosy, ebullient and mutton-chopped Max Gotch.

Putting on a cheery smile, he called out "Come right in, Mrs. Cameron, merry Christmas to you and the boy. Hark the herald angels sing!"

She entered the long narrow room with the teller's cage on the right, and moved close to an elegant tiled heating stove near the banker's desk. After taking a deep breath of relief Rose loosened Tommy's wraps, then sat in the chair Gotch courteously pushed forward.

"A real blue norther, isn't it?" the small man said, dropping a billet of wood into the stove. "How is everything out at the ranch?"

"Just fine, Mr. Gotch, except for that cold wind."

"Like they say down in Texas it only blows this way six months out of the year, then it turns around and blows the other way." Gotch said, laughing at his own humor.

Looking at solemn, hollow-eyed Tommy, he protested with a smile, "That's supposed to be a joke, boy!"

"I couldn't keep him out at the ranch in this weather, Mr. Gotch," Rose said.

"I don't suppose he hears many good jokes, so he doesn't know...." Gotch worried, moving to his chair behind the desk.

"Right now I need to borrow a few dollars for food and shelter." Rose said quietly.

"Things that bad?" Gotch asked, concerned.

"They'll get better," Rose said.

"I'm sorry Mrs. Cameron—it's not the money, it's the way banks operate. There are so many laws and regulations nowadays, a man can hardly tie his shoes without some government parasite telling him how to do it."

Pausing, he looked for a moment into her steady eyes, then shifted his gaze to the ceiling, "Still now—don't get the wrong idea, Rose, I could use a housekeeper, and we've been friends a long time...."

"Not that friendly!" Her face flushed with anger, Rose stood and spoke strongly. "If some poor man robs this bank and needs help getting away, I hope he'll come to me."

Gathering up Tommy, she went out the door. Gotch hurried after her, but the door slammed in his face.

"Females!" Gotch snapped in frustration. "No sense of humor."

Rose lumbered down the boardwalk in the near darkness watching the lamps being lighted through small frost coated windows, and coming to the corner, she turned right toward the gulch that marked the poor section of town.

In the distance she saw a small golden light gleaming in the wind whipped dusk, and she stumbled through the trash, not so much from Tommy's weight, but from carrying him about the streets with only moments of rest.

"I'm tired, mama."

"We're both a little tired, but we can't rest just yet."

She looked across the gulch and remembered the Reverend saying 'they'll cut your throat just for your shoes', paused, then hunched against the wind, both arms holding Tommy, she pushed on across the gulch until she came to the dimly lighted building that had obviously at one time been a barn and stable.

The storm obscured mercifully whatever moon and stars that might have given some light, but she knew the street of shacks and hovels, cold dens of cast-off people, a shanty town said to be filled with robbers and cutthroats and keeping a law of its own.

"There's no place else...." she said aloud.

Lettered on the lamplit window she read 'Ira's Bar 'n Grill'.

Her stiffened fingers fumbled on the door knob, and she felt like weeping for her weakness, but she forced her fingers to work, and turned the knob.

With her back to the door she saw half a dozen empty tables and a counter. She smelled coffee, stew, and fir boughs. Off in the shadows stood a simply adorned Christmas tree.

Coming out of the kitchen a heavily built man wearing a flour sack apron and a wooden pegleg looked at her questioningly for a moment.

Pegging to the counter, he called, "It's late, but come on in Missus! Don't be shy. Ain't nothin' to fear on a night like this except freezing your katookis off, beggin' your pardon, ma'am."

"Katookis?" Tommy repeated, wide eyed.

She stared more from the surprise of meeting a hearty, open-faced human for a change than any fear of being sandbagged for her purse.

"I'm Rose Cameron, and this is my son, Tommy," Rose said unsteadily.

"And I'm Ira Armsbury, and I'll bet you'd like a cup of hot coffee."

She saw the blue and red tattoos on his hairy forearms, and the neat patches on his shirt and pants.

"Here or at a table?" he asked anxiously, seeing that she hadn't put her bundled child down. "Please just sit down and take a load off your feet."

"Maybe the table is best," she murmured, unsure of herself.

He brought the coffee over to the table and pulled out a battered wooden chair for her.

"What's wrong with the little tyker?" he asked, touching Tommy's forehead with the tattooed back of his powerful hand. "Some fever, for sure."

She looked more closely at his stubbled features and saw that his broad forehead was deeply lined with three vertical grooves just over his big flattened nose. His wide cheekbones and heavy jaw made a generous mouth and a scar ran slantwise from his chin to his left ear. A shaggy mop of black hair tossed about as he moved his head, and in his amiable voice was the confidence that pleasant simplicity was the best answer to the world's troubles.

"You're carryin' a heavy burden, ma'am," he said, patting her on the shoulder with his big hand. "How'd you like a bowl of Ira's best Son of a Butcher stew?"

Rose tried to speak, but the shock of being suddenly offered hospitality when she needed it most, choked her throat, until in a high, quavering voice she said, "Folks always said never go across the gulch—they'll steal you blind and I don't know what all... now I'm here..." her voice faded into a weary whisper, "now I'm here... Mr. Armsbury, I can't pay you anything...."

As Rose fed Tommy from the bowl of rich beef stew, Ira came out from the kitchen and asked in his raspy voice, "Another helping, ma'am?"

"No thank you, Mr. Armsbury," Rose said, "I'm feeling a lot better."

Ira touched Tommy's forehead and asked, "How do you feel, mister?"

"Better," Tommy murmured, his eyes dull, his face flushed.

"He needs rest," Ira said, "and somethin' more than that."

"I bought a bottle of Santee's Croup Cure," Rose said, bringing the small bottle out of her bag.

Ira opened the bottle and sniffed at its contents. Wrinkling his big, fleshy nose with disgust, he rumbled, "This stuff is just alcohol, peppermint, and opium. It may put you to sleep, but it won't cure nothing."

The team bells attached to the front door jingled, and a young woman dressed in a shapeless dark blue coat pushed through. She had to lean against the door to shut it against the freezing wind.

"Jeee-sus, it's colder'n hell out there!" she exclaimed, brushing the snow off her coat and taking off a knitted stocking cap that revealed a brush of short cut red hair.

"Evening, Lena, this here is Mrs. Cameron and her boy, Tommy."

"Call me Rose, Lena," Rose said, seeing that she was hardly more than a girl with a slim figure and a round, gamin face freshened by the wind and snow.

Lena smiled at Rose, and looked down at the boy. "What's the matter, Tommy, can't wait for Christmas?"

Then she noticed his flushed cheeks and vague eyes, and automatically touched his forehead. "Fever."

"That's why I brought him in from the ranch. I thought I could care for him better." Rose nodded.

Tommy looked up at Lena, and wheezed, "Pretty hair."

"Aw," Lena laughed and patted his thin shoulder. "You sound like every other boy I ever knew."

Suddenly Tommy's eyes bulged as he fought for air and his lungs produced a series of hacking whoops alternated by the whistling intake of quick breaths.

Lena dropped to her knees and wrapped her thin arms around his chest and held him tight until the coughing ceased.

"He ought to be in bed, Rose," Lena said anxiously.

"We'll be all right," Rose said, rising. "Thanks again for everything."

Lena looked over at Ira's heavy features, then back to Tommy's feverish face.

"My room's in back.... it's clean," she said. "You take it, Rose."

"I can't take your bed on a night like this," Rose said positively. "I'm much obliged for your kindness, but there must be someplace—"

"Across the gulch?" Lena chuckled. "There's places, but not for you, lady."

"I don't understand."

"Just as well." Lena stood up. "Ira gives me a room and you're going to use it and make me feel good about myself."

Chuckling, she led Rose back through the kitchen to a bedroom at the rear of the building, and lighted a lamp.

"Ain't nothing fancy," Ira said. "Was a stable before Lena fixed it up. I bunk up in the hayloft if you need anything ma'am."

The former stable was plenty big enough to hold an old iron bed, a bench, two chairs, and a bureau. On the walls were magazine illustrations pasted in neat rows. At the rear was a small door.

"That door goes out back," Lena said. "Just keep it barred unless you want to go out."

"But what about you?" Rose protested.

"Like I said, I can find a spare bed a lot easier'n you can," Lena smiled mischievously, making her own kind of joke. "I want this young man to get back on his feet and take me dancing."

"I don't know how to thank you, Lena," Rose said, fighting back tears of gratitude. "Ira, I mean to pay—"

"Later. Right now we got to fix up Tommy and get set for a new baby, important things. Goodnight, Mrs. Cameron," Ira said, going out the door.

"Call me Rose," the big, weary woman said softly, but Ira was gone.

"I'll be back first thing in the morning," Lena said. "By then maybe the storm'll be over and we can help Ira. He doesn't complain, but his leg gives him a lot of pain when he walks, especially when it's cold."

"Will you be all right, Lena?" Rose asked, searching the girl's face with worried eyes.

"Don't worry. Little Lena McCoy has lots of friends in town...." The redheaded gamin laughed, and backed out the door, leaving Rose to herself.

Rose shook her head in wonder and sat down on the pine bench to remove her boots. Then, shedding her woolen coat, she blew out the lamp and crept into the blankets beside the sleeping boy.

She felt the life shift inside her as the polar winds slammed against the wooden walls, and showed no signs of abating. She touched her great taut abdomen and said, "Please, little child, you've got to wait."

As Nellie Damker skimmed the thick cream from the milk bucket, she heard the Colonel's snoring in the next room broken by an occasional groan of pain which she knew came from the shattered bones in his left shoulder where a minie ball had smashed through and never healed properly.

Stubbornly he never mentioned it to anyone except her, and he gave her strict orders that she was not to speak of it to anyone, not even his sons.

No one knows, she thought, that he stands so straight because he can't do anything else. Had the boys known, maybe they'd been more tolerant of his stiff necked ways. Maybe if I hadn't known he was covering up that pain all the time, I would have gone along with them.

Even after they'd married he'd tried to hide it by wearing a flannel nightshirt to bed, but it wasn't long before she saw his long body naked early one morning, saw the cratered scar in the front of his shoulder and the odd lumps of mismatched fractures poking against the skin on his back.

It wasn't that he was ashamed of being wounded. After all, he'd gained a promotion for his courage, but he felt it diminished his standing amongst men, and what they didn't know wouldn't hurt them.

"It's nobody's business but my own, woman!" he'd said strongly, and she had abided by his wishes

If he wanted to look like a hard hearted, unbearable tyrant, then he'd surely succeeded, but she didn't really believe he saw himself that way. More likely, he thought strength and discipline and hard work were civilized virtues that should be known by his example.

Pouring the cream into the salt glazed butter churn, already half full, she thought she'd better make butter in the morning.

They already had enough butter to last until spring, but the cream was there to be used and she could trade the butter to Mr. Veiten in Calico for flour and sugar. Waste not, want naught, she thought.

Thinking of sugar and hard times and what the Colonel had said about the Widow Cameron, her mind went to a tragic incident that had occurred last fall up on Cherry Creek where a young couple was trying to make their home against impossible odds.

The husband had returned in the late afternoon to find his wife hanging from the windmill that had quit working two weeks before.

After he'd cut her down, he looked through the one room cabin for some clue to her suicide and could find only a few jars of runny jelly by the stove. It was a puzzle until he recalled that she'd had trouble getting the half wild cow milked, then the cream wouldn't clabber for cheese and wouldn't clot to make butter, and the sourdough bread wouldn't raise right, then she'd tried to make wild berry jelly but it wouldn't jell.

If she'd only had a little patience, Nellie thought sadly, if she'd just come over and asked me... I'd a told her she needed more sugar for the jelly, a spoonful more sugar for her sourdough starter, the cream would have clabbered if she'd kept it warm, or made butter if she'd...

But she was too shy to ask. Turned out she had no shoes. Couldn't go ask a neighbor how to make jelly barefooted.

Poor child.... Buried barefoot, and the husband next day rode away.

Such a hard country, she thought. So much to learn, and so many hopes and expectations you've got to put aside. I wish now I'd taken time to go visit the girl, but the Colonel said they were squatters he was going to put the run on. Still, what difference if they were squatters, first of all they were human beings....

Anaberta moved about the big room, making sure the door was barred, the big chunk of mesquite firmly bedded on the coals in the fireplace so it couldn't roll out later on, and after rinsing the beans, she added water to the iron pot and put it hanging on a hook near the fire where they'd soak and stay warm during the night.

She thought she should start getting ready for the kids' Christmas. Although they wouldn't open their presents until the night of the Wisemen, January sixth, she should have buñuelas and biscochitos and the dulce de calabaza ready for the nine Posadas evenings before that.

It was these events that made the life even out here enjoyable. If people were lazy or forgot the holidays, then it was just one tonto day after another, but if there was always a fiesta coming, you could be happy just preparing for it.

She wondered if the people ever celebrated anything or had a fiesta in Calico. It seemed ever time she went for supplies, all she ever saw were worriers thinking more about working than playing. In that way, her mother-in-law was right about the Anglos. They acted like having fun was a sin.

Well, that's their business, she thought. Thank the good Lord I enjoy taking care of the kids and playing their games with them.

When I know they are clean and well fed and happy, then I am happy.

Hilo y aguja, media vestidura! Thread and needle, half the dress. Better if they had other friends to play with. Sooner or later they will have to talk to others outside the family. Each one will want to be different, she thought, and they'll have to learn that there are many ways to be different. Better for them if they could see that some people were honest and happy and some people were not honest and had strange ideas about happiness.

True, she admonished herself, I'm the worst of all. I don't know anything except my family and 'Nato's family. How can I teach my children if I know nothing myself?

How nice it would be to have a neighbor close by, even a bad one would serve as an example of what not to be to the children.

Blowing out the last candle, she tiptoed into the smaller bedroom where Fortunato was already asleep.

Only through the one small window could she hear the storm blowing crazily. The rest of the house, being of earth and rock gave the gale no notice, and the room was quiet as a cave.

Thinking now about the widow woman just a few miles over the hills, she wondered if her house was so solid and pro-tective. Perhaps there were no rocks for building over there. Perhaps there were no steep-walled canyons to hold back the wind....

She hoped Fortunato was wrong, that there was grass enough for the lady's stock, that she would not have to leave her home and go away.

Maybe if things got too bad she and her little boy could come over and live with us, she thought. We could learn from each other. We have plenty of room and always enough to eat, why not?

A comadre, she would be like a sister to me, Anaberta thought warmly, and I could teach her how to make tortillas and she could teach me how to make white bread....

Waking in the near darkness, Rose almost cried out in panic when she couldn't remember where she was or how she got there until she felt the extra warmth of Tommy sleeping beside her.

Can't fall apart now, she admonished herself. Strange bed, strange room, strange place. No better or worse than out at the ranch, it's just different.

Then she remembered the norther and Tommy's fever and the stranger Joel Reese riding into the yard... a well set up man but troubled by some kind of an Irish black dog riding on his back, a sense of doom from his past, his manhood humbled by bouncing off too many unyielding brick walls, a lonely man....

Then the town, so paralyzed by poverty, cluttered, littered, fouled by trash, its essential heart festering from the decline of human pride and common decency....

Except Ira... who seemed to be the only man left with a heart of gold... a man who'd been everywhere and done everything and become the better for it... and somewhere in his long journey he had seen that life, was sharing, not taking, saw that it was action, not words, surely a diamond in the rough....

Listening to Tommy's hoarse, ragged breathing, she felt another surge of fear.

She'd lost Jim because she didn't know anything about doctoring, and here was Tommy getting worse every day and yet she didn't know why. She'd thought it was just a case of the croup, a cough and fever that would go away after a few days, but this seemed more deadly serious. Surely there ought to be some way to turn it around, but no one knew how. For sure, Doc Snarph didn't know. Tommy had rested and been warm all night, but if anything, the fever had gone up and his cough deepened.

"Mama...." Tommy murmured.

"I'm here, Tommy," she said, patting his shoulder.

"Is daddy in heaven?"

"I think so," she said. "It's hard to talk about because no one knows for sure about heaven."

"Are there angels?"

"Maybe...."

"That fly with wings?"

"The Bible says there's angels, but angels didn't write the Bible, different people did, and people can make mistakes or let their imaginations loose...."

"Why not have horses instead of wings?" Tommy asked weakly.

"I'm all for it," Rose said. "Makes more sense to me anyway."

"Maybe daddy is riding in heaven."

"Maybe," Rose nodded.

"But where would he ride to?"

"I reckon he'd ride over to the river," Rose said, a strange anxiety building in her heart.

"When I die, can I ride along with him?" Tommy asked in a painful whisper.

"Tommy, listen to me, you're not going to die from a little fever," Rose said firmly, "because I'm going to need your help one of these days."

"I don't know as I've got any say about it," Tommy said, frowning.

"Tommy," Rose said more strongly, "people... little boys don't lust die to go off to heaven. It's better if they spend a lot of time earning their way first."

"Everybody?"

"Some do, some don't—" she said, deeply troubled. "Some can, some can't, but everybody gets a try."

"Did daddy earn his way?"

"Yes, and he did well," Rose said softly, tears in her eyes. "But now that he's gone, it's up to us to build our own lives along the same lines but with different people and different experiences."

"I want to ride like him," Tommy said.

"You will, Tommy, you will," Rose said fervently.

"Mama, don't worry about me," Tommy said, closing his eyes.

Nellie Damker started the fire by blowing on splints of pitch pine she put on the embers still remaining in the firebox of the iron cookstove. Once she saw the flame, she added scraps of pinyon and mesquite until the fire roared up the tin chimney. When the draft was strong and the fire well started, she adjusted the damper on the stovepipe to hold the warmth inside. The iron stovetop crackled as it heated.

After she'd put the coffeepot on the stove, she paused to look out the narrow window to see what the night had left and the day would bring. In the crisp light of dawn she could see hard crusted patches of sleet here and there, but no heavy snow banks, certainly not enough to break the drought.

The wind had died down but it was still deadly cold outside.

It's one of those killer storms you don't know what it's going to do, she thought. Maybe it'll warm up with a Chinook, maybe it'll twist around and start blowing again worse than ever.

She heard the bedroom door open and close, and turned to see her husband buttoning a wool shirt, still half asleep. He hadn't shaved and she noticed the stubble on his cheeks was white as the sleet patches outside and thought with a pang of pity that he was too old to be working like a young rancher just getting started.

"Wind's down," she said, putting the big iron fry pan on the stove and peeking into the coffee pot to see if it was near boiling yet.

"Snow?"

"No more'n a bushel or two," she said, shaking her head.

"We don't get a big snow soon, the wells will go dry next summer—every damn well in the country," he muttered morosely.

"We been here forty years and it's never come to that," she replied.

"Half the winter's gone already," he countered somberly.

After putting a handful of ground coffee in the pot, she asked, "Did you ever think of just selling out?"

"Who would buy this place?" he countered, and answered his own question. "Nobody in his right mind. Price of cows is down so low it wouldn't pay to drive 'em to market.

Keep the stock here they'll all be buzzard bait. Price of hay's
out of sight. Add all that up—and what do you get?"

"We're not beat yet," she said, setting the coffee pot over
the cooler side of the stove, then spooning bacon grease into
the frying pan. "Suppose Mrs. Cameron would rent you her
range?"

"She don't cotton much to me," the colonel said evasively, "and I'm not about to beg."

"What have you ever done to make her hostile?" Nellie
asked, catching the change in her husband's tone of voice
like he was trying to slip something past her.

"Nothing that I know of," the Colonel said, shaking his
head, and added, "she blames me for a few head of cattle that
strayed off somewhere."

"Did they stray or did you push 'em?" Nellie demanded,
facing her husband.

"I am not accountable for her property," he came back at
her angrily. "You notice the Sheriff never came around asking
about her cattle, and the reason for that is there's no evidence
of any wrongdoing."

"Where did they go?" she asked accusingly.

"How in tarnation would I know?" he growled. "They
could have been rustled by Fajardo. They could have been
driven over to Carson. They could be anywhere. It's up to her
to go looking, not me."

"It wouldn't hurt us none to help her look," Nellie said
stubbornly.

"Be sensible, woman," the Colonel said. "I didn't make
this drought. I didn't give her husband blood poisoning. I
didn't sic that slick hired hand onto her, and we've got
enough trouble ourselves without taking on somebody else's,

especially somebody who hasn't a chance in hell of coming through."

"So you figure it's more merciful to end her pain as soon as possible instead of her starving out slow," Nellie said grimly.

"That's it in a nutshell," he said. "And the fact is, I'm going to move some cattle over on to her west range today."

"She know about it yet?" Nellie asked, frowning.

"It don't make a nevermind. I'll pay her the rent out of what we sell the stock for next summer," the Colonel said. "Likely she won't even know they're there, what with her being pregnant and all."

"Pregnant!" Nellie shrieked in surprise. "Why didn't you tell me?"

"I figured you knew like everybody else," he said weakly.

"How can I know anything the way I'm cooped up here!" she retorted angrily. "I'm going to take the buckboard and see what she needs!"

"I wouldn't try it in this weather," the Colonel said slowly. "It's too late anyway."

Chapter Seven

Shrugging into his buffalo robe, Joel Reese strode outside in the early morning light and finished demolishing the turkey pen with the ax, then piled the last of the wood on the front porch. As he set the ax aside, he heard the bawling of cattle off to the west.

Standing by the open barn door, he wondered if his ears were playing tricks on him again.

She'd said her cows were gone and she only had a few hammer-headed mustangs grazing loose.

Whatever it was, it had to be looked into before he left, because if something came up missing, he didn't want to be blamed for it.

He smoothed the blanket over the black stud's back, hoisted up his single-fire hull, bridled the horse, and, leading him outside, mounted up.

He listened again. Cattle were moving up near the head-waters of the creek

He knew if he touched a spur to the stud's flanks, he'd buck and crowhop, and it was just too cold to fight. Instead, he gave the horse a gentle knee, pointed him northwest, and let him make his own pace until he'd worked the kinks out of his powerful muscles.

It was new range for him and frost covered the trails, forcing him to be wary of bad footing.

Fog blew from the nostrils of the big black as he tried an easy trot, his head coming up high, his tail swishing and the muscles in his shoulders weaving back and forth under Joel's left hand.

Joel pulled his hat brim down to shade his eyes from the glare and rode westerly until he saw the gaunt red and yellow and black critters up the valley between the cottonwoods that marked the creek bed and the fence line.

Strays, he thought, wind drifted 'em against the fence and they pushed on through.

As Joel drew closer he saw a pair of riders behind the small herd of cows. His eyes narrowed and his jaw set solid as he cut left. Though the riders had obviously seen him, they went on about their business of whacking their lassoes on the rumps of laggard cattle.

Both riders wore heavy canvas coats lined with sheepskin and mufflers tied around their necks underneath their wide brimmed hats. Keeping their legs warm were fleece lined chaps, and they wore leather mittens instead of gloves.

Without pausing, Joel Reese pushed the big black directly in between the rear rider on a shaggy grey gelding and the steer he was whipping, forcing him to pull up.

"Out of my way," the slope-shouldered rider with the long iron-gray mustache yelled.

"You're on Circle C ground," Reese said, not moving.

"And I'm from the Bar D next door. Who the blazes are you?"

"I'm takin' care of Mrs. Cameron's place. You best push your cows back home."

"Stay out of my business, cowboy," the old slope-shouldered rider snapped back.

The second rider on a ratty grulla mustang quit hazing the cattle and rode over to the right, keeping Joel whipsawed if trouble came.

"You know right from wrong," Reese said, tipping his hat brim up so that the rider could see his face. "If I have to set you afoot out here, I will, and I'll drive your critters back where they came from."

"Get the hell out of my way!" Damker roared.

"You're not listenin'," Reese said.

Awkwardly unbuttoning his canvas coat, the Colonel glanced over at his partner and said, "Ready, Shorty?"

Reese didn't wait for the rider to find his revolver under the coat. Touching the spurs to the black, he drove the stud hard against the grey, knocking him back on his haunches, and with a swing of his right arm, Reese swept the rider back over the mustang's rump. As the Colonel fell to the ground, the horse recovered his footing, lashed out with a rear hoof and ran back toward the west.

Reese turned to the smaller rider who was pawing at his coat buttons with his mittened fingers and making no progress.

"Go on, Shorty," Reese said patiently, "Push them cows back to their own pasture."

"There ain't nothin' for 'em to eat back there," the smaller rider said. "The Colonel said move 'em over here."

"I said push 'em back and fix that fence." Reese said harshly.

As Shorty rode off, Damker got to his feet and blustered, "You best fog out of this country while you're still able!"

"Why don't you try renting the pasture from the lady instead of stealing it?" Joel asked.

"Be better for her to just quit and get it over with. She can't ever make anything here," the Colonel said, trying to be reasonable.

"She could if she had decent neighbors," Reese said grimly.

"Maybe you don't know it, stranger," the Colonel said, "but there's a big flock of woolies over east that are set to move in. I'm just makin' my move first."

"You're beggin' the question about helpin' the lady," Reese said.

"It's dog eat dog out here, and I'm damned if I'm goin' to be beat out by a stinkin' sheepman!" Damker flared.

"I'll worry about the sheep, you mind your cows," Reese said, turning the black stud and seeing that Shorty had turned the cattle back onto the Bar D range, rode east.

Although the sun hadn't come through the icy grey overcast even yet, Nellie went ahead and baked a spice cake with raisins in it, did her chores, churned the butter and was ready before noon.

The two old winter shaggy horses in the corral were tame enough for her to harness to the buckboard, and after she'd packed the cake and a lard pail full of sweet butter in the back, she carried a couple of comforters to the seat just in case it got colder, and started the horses off at a walk.

Nellie wasn't exactly sure of the way, but in the early days she'd ridden alongside the Colonel and she remembered the Circle C was not too far off from the main road to Calico. It shouldn't be over seven miles.

Once the team had limbered up their muscles, she shook the reins and got them moving at an easy trot, and despite the barrenness of the countryside, she enjoyed being outside, on the move, and thinking of different things.

I've let myself become a hermit, she thought. Been so busy making work for myself, I've let Wayne do all the visiting and talking because he's out and around all the time. Still, I don't like his being flustered about Mrs. Cameron's cattle. Whatever he said wasn't all the truth. Something's cross-ways over yonder.

Coming to the fork in the road, she brought the team to a walk and reined them up the left hand branch. At first they were unwilling, being accustomed to going straight on into town, but keeping the pressure on the reins and barking her commands in a no-nonsense tone of voice, she quickly convinced them that she wasn't crazy and knew where she was going.

In half an hour the buckboard came to the open gate, and she again slowed the team to a walk while she observed the run-down condition of the ranch, the empty corrals and the absence of smoke from the chimney. There seemed to be no life anywhere.

Stopping the team in the yard, she called out, "Hello the house!" twice, but heard no response. Shivering from the stark loneliness of the scene, she stubbornly stepped up on the porch and knocked on the door.

"Mrs. Cameron, are you there?" she called out, knowing it was futile. There hadn't been a sound from the whole ranchstead since she'd arrived except the rising wail of the wind.

Again she called out just to be sure.

Peeking through a single pane window, she saw that the main room was clean and tidy, and definitely empty. If she'd known Rose Cameron at all she might have gone on inside and looked in the back bedroom, but she was in the unhappy position of being a stranger even to her next door neighbor.

She looked around again at the desolate yard and noticed a bush wrapped in burlap near the well. Probably a rose bush she cares about enough to try to keep it from freezing, she thought.

Nearby were the remnants of a summer garden, a patch of dried small stalks of corn blown down, withered tomato plants, white stalks of cabbages that had been cut off cleanly.

She's a worker, all right, Nellie thought, but no woman could keep this place up without some help. Sure, she's tryin' hard enough, but there's a man needed here. Not just any hired hand either, it'll take a man with sense enough to see the future is worth working for.

Climbing back into the buckboard, she was ready to start off when she saw the lonely marker on the knoll.

That'll be for her poor husband, Nellie thought, and clamped her lips together in a spasm of sympathy for the little family that had labored for their dream, and failed. She'd done the same labor and suffered similar hardships, the pain of accidents, and the weariness after a long day's haying in the August sun. She knew the heartbreak of seeing the dream almost come true but then failing from some whim of weather or circumstance. In that moment her heart went out to a woman she didn't really know well enough to talk to, but whose sister spirit she could see all around her and she knew that courageous and enduring woman as well as herself.

"Too late...." she said sadly to the horses, "she's gone. I let her down."

Anaberta quietly seated the sleepy child on the rocking chair and covered her with a lamb's wool blanket she had woven herself.

Next came the building up of the fire from embers of the night before.

As she moved about, she noticed that Ignacio had risen early, folded his blankets in a neat pile and had gone out to inspect the sheep.

Through the window she saw there had been little snow and the yard had been scoured clean by the twisting wind. Icicles hung from the eaves like clear ice roots and she knew it was still freezing outside.

As the fire gained strength she set the coffee pot on the hook over the flame, and busied herself chopping up a chorizo sausage which she put in an iron spider to fry, while she patted out more corn tortillas for breakfast. When the chorizo was cooked, she'd dump in a mixture of tomato sauce with mashed dried chilies and scrambled eggs and cook the whole meal in one pot.

Left over chorizo and salsa would go into the beanpot.

Soon the family would smell the rich flavors and the heated tortillas and would need no waking up call from her.

After grinding a handful of roasted coffee beans, she put the grounds in the simmering water and lifted the pot away.

Fortunato came in from the chilly bedroom carrying his boots and finished dressing in front of the fire.

"Ignacio?" he asked.

"Outside," she said quietly.

Moments later the children arrived in various states of dress, and she was kept busy buttoning buttons and buckling buckles, and seeing the right foot was in the right shoe.

Lastly came Fortunato's mother who took her customary chair by the fireplace, savoring a cup of strong black coffee, wisely keeping quiet and out of the way as the children commenced clamoring for breakfast.

All that was needed to settle them down was to dish out the chorizo omelet and put the plate of hot tortillas covered with a cloth to keep them warm in the center of the table.

"Will you eat, mama?" Fortunato asked politely.

"Later," his mother said as always.

He didn't ask Anaberta because it was understood she had to keep making and heating the tortillas.

When the children were finished eating, they drifted off to the far corner of the room where they'd built a corral of benches and sheep skins and started playing a make-up game of protecting the flock from coyotes and Indians.

Smiling, Anaberta cleared space for her mother-in-law and herself next to Fortunato and the two women settled down at the table for their own breakfasts.

Before they could start, Ignacio came through the door, stamping his feet, and Anaberta quickly set a place for him, too.

"Cold out there—so cold the air crackles like the trees were on fire," the small sheepherder said, shedding two patched coats.

"The flock?" Fortunato asked.

"They are no stronger." Ignacio said.

"Asi es la vida," the old woman said, nodding to herself.

"Can they walk to the Western range?" Fortunato asked.

"There's very little feed there." Ignacio shook his head.

"Maybe the widow Cameron would permit us to graze on her land a few days," Fortunato said.

"Have you talked to her?" Anaberta asked timidly.

"No, not since her hired hand left," Fortunato said. "She is not friendly to me."

"But you've done nothing to give her reason," Anaberta said loyally.

"I don't think so..." Fortunato said, looking away, "she had an idea that I might have been friendly with the man she hired, but I didn't even know him."

"It's the way they are," the mother said automatically.

"That was the man who came by here last summer on a big old stallion?" Anaberta asked, watching her husband's face.

"That was him," Fortunato said, "and I guess he stole the stallion, but it wasn't my fault."

"Didn't you buy some horses?" Anaberta questioned. "I remember.... There was something about money...."

"You're worrying your head about nothing," Fortunato said. "It's of no importance. I will take care of the ranch business and you may take care of the house business."

Before she could ask any more questions to dispel her doubts, Fortunato rose and said to Ignacio, "We'll put the sheep across the fence a short ways and what she doesn't know, won't hurt her."

"Fortunato..." she tried again, "Fortunato, are you sure you're doing the right thing?"

"I'm doing the best thing," Fortunato said heavily, and went outside with Ignacio following after.

Rose, fresh and rested came into the kitchen, and Ira offered her a mug of coffee.

"Good mornin', Ira."

"How's the little tyker this mornin'?"

"Better, maybe," she said, not telling all the truth, and looking into the empty dining room, she asked "How do you manage to stay open without any customers?"

"I've got enough customers," he smiled, ladling pancake batter on to a sizzling griddle, "but I only serve flapjacks, sourdough bread, and Son of a Butcher stew. That way my supplies are cheap enough to keep us all going."

"What do you put in the stew?" she asked.

"To make Son of a Butcher Stew," he grinned, "you throw everything in the pot except the hide, horns and beller."

"I want to help out," Rose said, tucking a dish towel around her waist.

"Maybe you can waitress some," Ira said, turning the bubbling flapjacks.

Stacking the flapjacks on the plate, he found a jar of sorghum molasses and a butter dish, and said, "There you are, ma'am. Your first waitressing will be to serve yourself."

She carried the tray into the dining room and sat at the counter with Ira pegging along behind.

"Delicious," she smiled. "I never knew I was so hungry."

"Eatin' for two does it," Ira smiled.

"How'd you learn to cook so well?"

"You might say I was forced into it," Ira chuckled. "After the Federal artillery was through with me, I wasn't much good for anything else."

An old man, nearly blind, wearing an overcoat much too big for him, tottered in through the door and made his way to the counter.

"Mornin', Ed," Ira boomed, going back to the kitchen. "How's your health and corporasity?"

"Some cold out there," the old man replied cheerily, "but the wind's dyin' down."

Rose carried her plate and cup back to the kitchen, then came back to the counter and said, "Good morning, Ed, what can I get you?"

"Eh?" Old Ed stared at her in confusion. "I don't need nothin', just coffee, ma'am. You new here?"

"Call me Rose, Ed," Rose offered cheerfully, pouring the coffee. "Yes, I'm trying to help out."

"Well, I'd say it's about time we had a pretty waitress," old Ed cackled. "Hear that, Ira? Hear?"

"Watch that old Billy goat, Rose," Ira called back. "He's known as Ready Eddie!"

Rose smiled, took the plate and, along with the butter and sorghum, placed it in front of the old man.

"I didn't order nothin'," old Ed protested, staring at the plate.

"You better eat it, or Ira'll give you a good talkin' to." Rose smiled, and heard the team bells on the door ring as an older woman came in the door and shuffled to the counter, eyeing Rose nervously.

"That's Sally Mae, Rose," Ira said, peering over the serving counter. "Coffee first."

"Good morning, Sally Mae," Rose smiled, putting the coffee and sugar bowl in front of the grey faced old lady.

"Mornin', ma'am, did Ira tell you... I can't—" Sally Mae's lips trembled and she stared at the floor.

"Don't worry about it, Sally Mae," Rose said gently. "We're all in the same boat."

A Paiute Indian dressed as a cowpuncher came in and quietly ordered flapjacks.

"Mornin', Pete," Ira called out. "Leadbellies comin' up."

A moment later, Lena came through the door and gave old Ed a friendly slap on the shoulder, and said hello to Sally Mae.

Looking over at Rose, she said, "You're lookin' pretty as a little red heifer in a flower bed this morning, Rose. How's Tommy?"

"No worse, Lena," Rose replied, putting a mug of coffee in front of her, then a stack of flapjacks.

"Darn it," the redheaded gamin frowned. "I was hoping a night's rest would help."

"It helped clear his lungs, but it's the fever that's up," Rose said.

"Freezin' out there," old Ed said, trying to make conversation. "not as bad as '53, of course...."

The Paiute Indian stood and put a silver dollar on the counter.

"Put this on my account, Ira," he called through the opening into the kitchen.

"Much obliged, Pete," Ira called back. "See you for supper."

Lena laid out another dollar and grinned. "I got an inheritance in the mail last night."

Rose frowned, trying to make sense of Lena's joking, then gave up as a couple of Mexican charcoal burners came in for their breakfast. Their clothing was blackened and they smelled of mesquite smoke.

"Mornin', gents," Ira called to them.

"Buenos dias. Ira," the first one said. "Today there is no money, but tomorrow we pay, 'sta bien?"

"'Sta bien," Ira boomed back, "and if you happen to find a stray goat or some fresh marrow bones, we can use them."

"Mañana, for sure," the carbonero smiled.

As people drifted in and out, Rose swabbed the tables and counter, put the dishes in a boiler on the stove, and Lena, carrying her own plate out to the kitchen, said, "You're a fast learner, Rose."

"I like sharing, but I just don't understand how Ira can afford it," Rose confessed, sitting down.

"Most of these folks will find work in the spring, and they'll ante up, and more. Some of them, like old Ed, won't ever make a dime, but Ira doesn't worry about it."

"Mama?" came the voice of Tommy from the bedroom.

Chapter Eight

"*I*'m here," Rose assured the boy.

"What do you want for Christmas, buckaroo?" Lena smiled.

Tommy closed his eyes without answering.

"His daddy promised him a hand made saddle his size. You know—with stampings and a wrapped horn, and double rigged...." Rose murmured.

"Wouldn't hurt to order it, there's still time," Lena said.

"But there's no money!" Rose cried out in despair.

"Now don't curdle your milk, Rose Cameron," Lena said, getting to her feet and going to the door. "Listen to me lady," Lena added, turning back to Rose, "you've got to think hopeful or you'll have an unhappy baby, and we don't want that."

"No, Lena, no we don't," Rose said softly, nodding her head with renewed determination, as Lena went out the door.

"When can we go back home?" Tommy asked weakly.

"Soon as you're well. And we're going to order that new saddle and a good pinto pony for you, and let you ride the range like the wind."

He looked up at her gravely and said, "No, you're makin' it up."

Rose pulled the comforter up to his chin, and said, "Rest easy, cowboy," then kissed him on his hot, dry forehead.

Back in the kitchen, Rose saw Ira hunched over a bucket, peeling potatoes. The stew meat was already seared and the iron skillet pushed back to the far side of the range.

"I've got a notion, Ira....," Rose said hesitantly.

"Don't be bashful," Ira laughed, "shoot."

"That hot oven is goin' to waste. If I could make up a batch of cookies, maybe I could sell 'em up town and start earnin' my way."

"You already earned your way, Rose." Ira dropped a peeled potato into a pail of clear water. "But if you want to sell cookies, there's flour and spices, maybe even a few raisins."

"Any rolled oats?"

"That's horse feed," Ira laughed. "Sure, there's almost a whole sack. You're sure you don't want to set around enjoyin' mornin' sickness?"

"There isn't time," Rose said, finding a big crockery bowl that would serve for mixing.

Joel Reese kept the black on good ground as the wind dropped to fitful breezes and thin snow formed a hard crust in the sub zero cold even though a pale wraith of sun stood overhead.

Damker wants to use up every last blade of grass for fear it'll go to waste, Reese thought. Don't know that nothin' goes to waste, it all gets used up for the best if you leave it alone.

At the upper northwest corner, he saw that the corner post had been set solid and then double braced against the next posts.

A good man did that, he thought. He took the extra time to do it right....

The thin patches of crusted snow crunched underfoot as the black stud moved easterly along the fence line, gradually going down hill toward a broad bottom land on either side of the meandering creek.

Protected by a thick belt of sycamores, the ground on the other side was almost bare of snow and a few mustangs were pawing through the icy shell for the good grass beneath.

He noted the Circle C brand on their near hips and saw that they were all mares in foal. Short coupled, hammer-headed, they were no doubt tough as wild horses, but there was little quality in their conformation, and only animal cunning in their narrow heads.

Reckon he had to use whatever was around, Reese thought. Maybe with a good Morgan stud, they might throw some fair looking colts come spring. It'd been better though, if the feller who rustled the best of the herd had taken them all and let the widow Cameron start off fresh.

The small, winter shaggy mares were wary, ready to bolt, but Reese kept his distance and crossed the creek at a ford covered with crackling ice, then continued on easterly, climbing from the bottom pasture land.

A jackrabbit blew out from under the stud's hooves and bounded off in mindless zigzags.

Reese considered he might make a fair stew, but he had no desire to chase or kill anything just now in the purity of the frosted landscape.

He looked back down at the mares grazing in the bottom land and began to understand that the vision of Jim Cameron was not much different than his own, except that Cameron had gone ahead and almost made it come true, instead of drifting on over the next mountain.

Cameron was a horseman, not a cattle or sheep man, and he'd seen how the creek and the bottom land could be used efficiently for a horse breeding and training operation better than for either sheep or cattle.

Of course a stud farm took a lot of extra time to turn out mature, well trained horses, but a small herd could be managed, each animal cared for, rather than just punching a herd of wild cattle or sheep.

It took money to find the best stock, the enduring Morgan, the intelligent Barb, and the Steeldust short sprinter combination, and breed up a line to your liking.

He'd dreamed this dream down in San Antonio before the war, and it had gone the way of all his other dreams of home, wife, kids, ranch, friends.

By the time the war was over, the girl he'd been keepin' his eye on since they'd first met in a brush arbor school house out west of San Antonio had produced two daughters by an older rancher and she looked like a cotton picker's sack half full. After that, he stayed clear of females, and drifted along with Jeff.

The folks' ranch had been lost to a carpetbagger banker. Friends were all dead in the war, and he couldn't find the money for raising horses for people who appreciated good riding stock.

All except for the black stud he'd bought as a colt four years back and gently schooled with the hackamore and soft hobbles, knowing he'd be safer if he cut him, but always holding back as he watched the stallion grow stronger into the conformation he admired most.

Likely Jim Cameron had owned a stud and used him to start his horse ranch, but that horse was probably in Mexico or Montana by now, being used by someone who never would know he was stolen from a widow woman down in the middle of Nevada...

There was enough hill country here to build up a colt's stamina, and enough bottom land to keep him growing without dry, hunger spells in between.

There were the constant spring fed water holes so you weren't always fighting alkali or bogs.

No darn wonder everybody wanted it.

Continuing on up the rise, he saw that he was coming to the topmost range, the bulging hill overlooking the whole ranch, as well as the ramparts to the west and the rocky foothills to the east. On south were the ranch buildings, nestled in their own sheltered swale, then the wagon trace running off toward town so far away he couldn't see it even in the clear crisp air, except as a smudge of pale grey smoke and an irregular skyline where he hoped Rose and Tommy Cameron were safe and well.

A wondrous thrill ran through his long body and choked his chest as he thought of Rose and Tommy and saw the whole layout in its simple completeness, the hills for space to run in, the bottom land for pasture and hay, the water, the ranchstead, all ready to start over again, the dream of any horseman who knew his way and was willing to work at it.

So much different than the lonely life of the drifter!

Yet it was, after all, just a dream that had nothing real in it for a penniless wanderer. His thoughts shifted and his heart went out to the man who had dreamed it and almost done it, Jim Cameron. How he respected that man, though he'd never met him! His plan and purpose were everywhere and his presence was in every one of those well set posts, in the layout of the spread, in the stubborn determination of his good wife to hold on to that dream for the boy and the baby yet to come.

It was a powerful emotional moment for him as he sat the big black horse and surveyed what might have been a small paradise for a good man if he'd just lived to finish it. Jim Cameron had had everything but good luck.

Shaking his head, but not complaining about his own fated years, he kneed the big black on east toward the rocky country.

The ground had been too shallow to plant the corner post to the thirty inches Jim Cameron wanted, and unable to dig through the sandstone, he'd rolled big rocks onto the corner, making a cairn around the post so that it wouldn't bow one way or the other.

On across the fence, bunch grass grew thinly among the rocks which would support sheep, but be difficult for cattle or horses.

Accordingly, the sheepman had tried to use it the best way he knew.

Reese could see though, that what with the drought and too many hungry mouths, most of the grass had been nibbled down to the coarse dirt, and that spelled trouble.

Down below he saw a flock of grayish white sheep being crowded close to the fence by a pair of black and white border collies, and a herder backing them up.

Next to him a rider on a tall sorrel urged them on.

Mesh fencing might have held the sheep to their own range, but the four wire fence wouldn't stand the crowding of small animals and some were already being pushed through willingly enough toward the relatively ungrazed Circle C range.

Reese kneed the black into a headlong gallop down the slope, giving a raucous "Hold it!" as he charged the fence, sending the sheep off in a panic despite the frantic efforts of the dogs to hold them.

Seeing the flock scattered on down their hill, Reese put the black to herding the half dozen sheep that had come through the wire back uphill to the corner where he dismounted and, leaving the black to keep them cornered, waded into them, seized their fleeces and lifted them one by one, back over the fence.

Blatting and looking for their mates, the half dozen strays were rounded up by a dog on a hand signal from the herder and put back in the flock.

As the tall, slim rider on the sorrel approached the fence, Joel mounted up and rode closer.

Joel saw that the well dressed rider was a Mexican with a trim mustache and wary eyes. He wore a woolen coat with silver buttons and soft black calfskin boots.

There was a grim fatalism in the rider's brown eyes which seemed to say he could be pushed plenty far, but when he reached his limit, he'd die fighting back. He came forward without fear or threat, simply coming to see what the big man had to say.

"Buenos dias, senor," the rider said.

'Buenos dias. Com' esta?"

"Bien gracias, y usted?"

"Mas o menos," Reese waggled his right hand back and forth. "Hablas English?"

"One must," the Mexican nodded. "My name is Fortunato Fajardo Pelayo. I own this land."

"My name is Joel Reese, and I don't want your sheep over here," Reese said carefully.

"The lady is now yours?" Fajardo asked.

"No, she's gone to town until the storm blows over."
Reese's face flushed from the unexpected question. "But I'm
here and if you crowd any more sheep over here, I'll pen 'em
up and sell them back to you."

"They're worth nothing," Fajardo chuckled.

"But this grass is worth something, and I aim to keep it
for the horses," Reese said with finality. "Comprende?"

"I don't take warnings from vagos," Fajardo said curtly.

"This old vago comes lookin' for you, you'll change your
mind."

Each man eyed the other, neither backing off until the
herder with the dogs yelled, "Vamos a las cuevas!"

Fajardo looked over his shoulder, shrugged, and said,
"Another time."

Anaberta heard her husband's horse coming into the
yard, and opening the door, she called out, "Hola querido
mio, you are back so soon to cheer up this cold day."

"Just for a minute," Fortunato said shortly, coming
through the door and without pausing to greet the children,
hurried on into the bedroom.

When he returned, he wore the black gun belt with the
pearl handled Colt revolver holstered on his right hip.

Anaberta saw the anger on his rigid features, and asked
timidly, "Please, Fortunato, tell me what has happened?"

"Nothing. Don't worry," he said. "It's just that the one
time I needed my gun, I left it home."

"Where are the sheep now?" she asked.

"Nacho has moved them south near the old caves, he
will hold them there."

"But he can't stay there all night!"

"Why not?" Fortunato smiled. "He has tortillas and beans. The caves are shelter enough. There is still a little grass down that way."

And you?

"I'm going to Calico to talk with Mrs. Cameron," Fortunato replied patiently. "Believe me, I'm not looking for trouble, but if she is leaving the ranch, I must know about it before Bar D."

"Are you sure she's gone to town?"

"Only the word of a cowboy she left in charge. If I'd had my gun..." he muttered, "but, I didn't."

"Why would she go to town in this kind of weather" Anaberta persisted.

"Because she is very, very pregnant, mi vida." Fortunato smiled again. "With her little boy, I suppose she thought it best to have the baby where people could help."

"Please be careful with the gun," Anaberta said, looking at him, her eyes shining, close to tears. "I worry—"

"I am not a fool with a gun, you know."

"Yes, I know you are a master, perhaps the best in the world, but it's better pasar la mano por le lomo," she said. "Better a pat on the back than a bullet."

"Por supuesto," he said agreeably. "Of course."

"May I go with you, mi valiente?" she asked. "I would like to speak with the Mrs. Cameron myself."

"It is not necessary," Fortunato shook his head, and kissing her quickly, turned and went out the door.

"What is this?" her mother-in-law asked. "I don't understand."

"Neither do I, mama," Anaberta said, frowning. "It all makes sense except why would he want the gun?"

"What makes sense?" the old woman snapped, "start at the beginning."

"He said Mrs. Cameron of the Circle C had gone to town to have her baby, and he wanted to talk with her."

"Yes, tienes raison," the old woman said, "the gun doesn't make sense."

"Mamacita, please can you look after the children while I'm gone?"

"I raised a dozen," the old woman said shortly, "you only have four."

"I'm trying to do better, mama," Anaberta smiled, and hurriedly donned her sheepskin overcoat.

"Can I go, mama?" Pedro called out.

"No, my love," Anaberta said at the doorway, "not this time."

Chapter Nine

"Christmas cookies?" Rose called out cheerfully to a gray-clad middle-aged couple trudging down the littered boardwalk. "Two for a nickel."

The couple looked furtively at her as if she might be carrying the plague, and hurried on, speaking in undertones to each other.

Dressed in her woolen coat and wearing woolen stockings, she paced heavily back and forth in front of the Mercantile, an oval shaped basket covered by a white towel hanging from her arm.

She'd been there an hour, and had yet to make a sale.

She'd thought it was a good enough idea to bake and sell the cookies and earn a few dollars. Maybe even make enough to buy Tommy's saddle, if she were lucky. But the town of Calico seemed to close in on itself because of the drought and cold.

"Cookies, Christmas cookies!" she called to a teenage boy scuffling his oversized, cobbled up boots through the muck.

"Lady, don't you know there ain't a nickel in this whole town!" the youth retorted angrily, as if it were her fault he had no mittens and had to bury his hands inside his ragged coat sleeves to keep them warm.

"Cookies, Christmas cookies, two for a nickel, twelve for a quarter!" she sang out to a ranchman riding by on a ribby mustang.

"Can't even feed my pony hay," the rancher said, and rode on dejectedly.

She stamped her feet to bring circulation back into her numb toes, and felt a painful needling in response.

She wouldn't be able to stay out much longer, and thought how disappointed Ira and Lena would be if she came back with her basket full.

"Say, Mrs. Cameron, say there...." George Veiten called to her from the doorway of his store, "maybe better you go by the bank. I'm trying to run a business and my customers you're scarin' away."

"Sure thing, Mr. Veiten," Rose responded with a smile. "I'm not exactly being run down by a stampede of hungry cookie lovers here—"

Crossing the street she called out to a young man dressed in a suit, overcoat, and derby hat, hurrying as if he were due at an important meeting.

"Cookies! Christmas cookies—"

"No thanks, lady."

"Two for a nickel!"

The young man turned his pale face away, ashamed that he hadn't a spare nickel in his pocket.

"Cookies, Christmas cookies!" she called out as Doctor Snarph drove by in his blue painted hack with its bright red wheels, the handsome chestnut Hambetonian drawing the hack with a smooth, measured trot.

The doctor seemed to shrink down inside the fox pelt robe that was drawn up over his knees.

"Good mornin', Doc," she called, refusing to be put off by his frosty attitude. "Two bits a dozen!"

"Haven't time—emergency..." Doctor Snarph responded, snapping his whip over the chestnut's withers. "Man over in the Gabilans nearly froze to death last night."

The bank door opened and Max Gotch came down the steps dressed in a grey wool suit and matching cape.

"Care for a bag of cookies, Mr. Gotch?" Rose forced a smile.

Gotch stopped at the foot of the steps, shook his head and grinned, "Like the cat said to the canary, you ought to be inside out of the cold, Mrs. Cameron."

"Like the canary said to the cat, Mr. Gotch, 'I've got to sing for my supper'." Rose smiled.

She put the basket over her right arm, and slapping her left hand against her thigh to bring warmth back to it, walked ponderously across the street to where the two story Plaza Hotel stood like a large grey box, its windows obscured with ice and frost, its central chimney giving off a thin plume of smoke.

"Cookies, Christmas cookies!" Rose called to Elroy Morrison as he drove four horses hitched to his heavy dray up the street.

"Can't afford such extravagance," he retorted, slapping the reins. "It's hard enough to find drinkin' money."

"Don't worry, Mr. Morrison," she called back, "you'll find it."

"What on earth is going on out here?" came the sharp voice of Ophelia Masson from the hotel doorway.

"Good morning, Mrs. Masson," Rose addressed the corpulent hotel keeper. "Care for a dozen cookies, fresh baked and only twenty-five cents?"

"I can't lose any weight eating cookies, Rose," Mrs. Masson protested gloomily

"Feed 'em to Mr. Masson. He's thin as a bell rope," Rose said, chuckling.

"What are you going to do with the baby when it comes?" Mrs. Masson asked, her voice softening.

"I'm going to raise him up on the ranch. Why?" Rose answered.

"Me and Elijah could help out. We can't have a child of our own, but we're not much against adopting one."

"My baby?" Rose exclaimed as if she hadn't understood.

"We could find you a nice room," Mrs. Masson said wistfully, "It'd be better'n having the fatherless baby in a barn, and we could do right by the child, teach him, and raise him up right."

"Ma'am, I understand how you must crave a child of your own, but mine are too precious to give away," Rose said sympathetically. "Thanks anyway."

"Don't be too hasty, Mrs. Cameron," Ophelia Masson said, trying to hide her disappointment. "Please just give it some thought."

"The answer would be the same tomorrow as it is today," Rose said. "I can't think of a thing that would change my mind."

"Suppose—" Ophelia Masson said softly, "just suppose you had an accident You have no relatives out here, and you've chosen to work on your ranch instead of making friends or joining the Fellowship. We all know that and don't hold it against you, but now with another little one, most anything could happen...."

"Like what?" Rose asked, trying to get ready for what the heavy-set woman would say.

"Oh, for example, say your team ran away and your buckboard turned over—say you slipped on the ice and broke a leg, or come down with the cholera, there's all kinds of terrible accidents happening every day...."

"All right," Rose nodded slowly, "go ahead supposin'."

"Well... it's just that I'd always be here to help out. A friend indeed. Someone you could depend on no matter what. You'd always have a safe harbor here in Calico," Ophelia said, her voice cracking with emotion.

"I'm sorry Mrs. Masson," Rose said, shaking her head, "I want you for a friend, but I can't live my life 'supposin' there's a calamity around every corner."

"You don't have to make up your mind right away," Ophelia said, trying to keep the thread of hope intact.

"Let's just suppose we're all good friends, looking after each other and enjoying everyone's company," Rose smiled. "I'd like that."

Crossing to the fourth side of the square in front of the Calico Queen Saloon, Rose called out to the empty trashy street, "Cookies, Christmas cookies!"

A man approached, so bundled up in sweaters and coats and scarves she didn't recognize him at first as the pastor of the Four Square Temple, Reverend Chamberlain, carrying a bible in his mittened hand.

"Cookies, Christmas cookies!" Rose did her best to roust up some cheerfulness in her voice. "Two for a nickel, Reverend."

The Reverend seemed not to hear, and Rose thought perhaps the double scarf wrapped around his head was blocking out her voice, and she stepped closer and spoke louder, "Care for a dozen cookies, Reverend?"

"Some other time," the Reverend said absently, coming out of his daydream. "Odd I was thinking off something important but I forget what it was.... How is our little boy?"

"Not much change. He's sleeping," Rose said.

"Where did you spend the night?"

"With friends," Rose said, smiling.

"I knew you would find a place," the Reverend said, nodding. "Calico has always been a friendly town."

"I had some doubts last night, and now I'm wondering about those horses—" Rose said gesturing at the hitch rail. "You recognize those brands?"

"The big grey is a Bar D," the Reverend said, glancing at the horses. "The next three mustangs aren't branded... and the sorrel on the end belongs to that sheepman over in the hills. Isn't it odd that so many shepherds become mystical prophets?... 'the pastures are clothed with flocks; the valleys are also covered with corn; they shout for joy, they also sing'...."

"I guess you wouldn't know trouble if it put a gun to your head, Reverend," Rose said, frowning. "Excuse me, I've got to get over to the livery barn right quick."

"But... but..." the Reverend stammered, "what is the problem?"

"Never mind, Reverend," Rose said, over her shoulder, "you go right on with your cogitations, I'll take care of it."

Joel Reese, big and somber as a cedar tree, had seen the lay of the land, and satisfied, rode back to the ranch house.

He'd seen the mends in the fence where it had been cut, stock driven out and patched back together again, and he understood how a few head of cattle and the best of the horse herd had disappeared, stolen, not only by Rose's hired hand. Likely the cattleman on the west and the sheepman on the east had appropriated some for themselves, probably not to acquire more stock, but more than likely to ruin Rose Cameron as quickly as possible in the name of mercy.

Each of them considered the Circle C as their ground because of the bottom grass and constant water,. Why should a simple widow woman own this remote place when it was so needed now to make the sheep ranch or the cattle ranch complete?

After awhile, he supposed, those men could figure they were doing her a favor to force her out so that it wasn't such a painful, dragged out struggle for her.

A man's mind worked in strange ways when he saw the value of neighboring land after it was too late to take it.

Putting the black in the barn with the three white turkeys, he dumped the rest of the sprouted potatoes into the feed trough, and, going toward the house, wondered what Rose Cameron would say when she saw that he'd used her turkey pen for firewood.

Probably get some salty about that, but he'd be long gone and forgotten soon enough.

In the kitchen, he opened the damper and got the fire going again, because even though the wind had died, the sun had never poked through the freezing clouds and outside the temperature had not yet risen to zero.

Hanging the buffalo robe on its peg by the door, he moved the skillet filled with the cold corndodgers over to the firebox side of the stove.

He'd promised the widow woman he'd leave as soon as the weather cleared, and, cold as it was, there was nothing to keep him here any longer.

Once the skillet was empty, he'd be heading west where there might be a need for a lone rider down on his luck. Someday, if he could ever make a stake, maybe he'd ride back over here and see how Rose was getting along. Maybe, if he had on a new outfit and was fresh barbered and smelled like a petunia patch, she might not throw rocks at him, might even take a liking to him....

Smiling at his own whimsy, he idly went though a small pile of magazines, recipes, a tally book, another hard bound notebook where the records of horses bought and sold had been entered.

First mentioned was Ben Bolt, grey stud, half Morgan, half Arab, fifteen hands, sixteen years old, still productive.

That old stud must have been the keystone of Jim Cameron's horse herd, Joel nodded thoughtfully. Some studs were still potent sires up in their twenties.

On down, Joel read of blooded mares, bought cheap from being lame, blind in one eye, ganted down, things that would make them useless except as broodmares, where the value of bloodlines could be exploited.

A wonder anyone even bothered to steal them, he thought, except of course, they'd all been in foal to the big stud, and would show their value when they foaled.

Beneath the record book of the stud, he found a worn tack circular from a saddle maker over in Carson named Durby.

The worn pages were illustrated with printed drawings of many styles of saddles. Breaking down the saddle into its various components, starting with a variety of wooden trees with high or low cantles, swell fork or a slick, gourd horn or iron, it showed how you could pick whatever parts you liked best and Mr. Asa Durby promised to put them all together for you at a base price of twenty dollars, unless of course, you wanted silver conchas, or special basket stamping, or hand carving of the leather, which cost more.

Curiosity aroused, Reese studied the order form and found that someone wanted a rig with a Spanish-American tree with a narrow swell fork and low cantle. He wanted a Sam Stagg double rigging with latigos, a plain saddle skirt and fenders with box stirrups.

Reese noted that the measurement of the various parts were unusually small, but only when he saw the seat was to be just two hands wide did he realize it was to be a child's saddle.

No doubt Tommy Cameron had studied the wish book for some time, changing this for that, back and forth, wearing out his eraser and the order form, too, until he put together what he thought would be the perfect saddle for himself.

He smiled at what must have been a great labor of love for the boy and remembered his own first saddle which had been built on the home ranch by old Anselmo.

He'd carved the tree from a chunk of cottonwood and then covered it with wet rawhide laced tightly. When the rawhide had shrunk in the sun, the tree was hard and strong. After that it was covered with a rectangle of soft cowhide split at both ends to fit around the cantle and horn.

Then he'd made it a center fire rig by hanging iron rings from either side for the stirrup leathers, and another ring underneath for the cinch's latigo.

It looked like a toy, but the old vaquero had put as much care into building it as he had put into his own, and when he first set it up on the smallest, gentlest horse on the ranch, everybody laughed, but then when young Joel stood on a fence rail and climbed on, it fit fine and after they'd adjusted the stirrups' length, he put the pony into a gallop out the ranch gate and scared poor mama half to death.

He must've been about six or seven then, about the same age as Tommy, and though he'd forgotten most of that time in his growing up, he could still recall every detail of that little saddle and his feeling of gratitude to Anselmo.

Things like that were important to little boys, he thought, probably more important than most folks realized.

You see a boy daydreaming over a saddle wish book and you smile and shake your head, but you don't really understand how important it is for the boy to see his dream come true.

Yet here was the order form not even torn out of the circular, never mailed with a twenty dollar bill to Asa Durby, saddle maker, Carson, Nevada.

He felt sick when he looked at the date at the top of the form, April 5.

Jim Cameron had been alive then. No doubt Tommy had asked which was better, a cantle backsloped, or a plain low cantle? Double rig or center fire? Iron horn or rawhide wrapped wood, California wood box stirrups or Texas iron?

A couple weeks later and the dream of settin' his own saddle and ridin' the range alongside his dad were gone forever.

That's a hard way to learn the lesson of failed dreams, he thought, but it happens to everyone, and there's no easy way to get around it.

Smelling char, Reese rose up from the table, pulled the skillet off to the cooler side of the stove top, and moodily chewed on a warmed over dodger.

Reluctantly, he shrugged into the buffalo robe and carried his bedroll out the door.

Going back to the table, he wrote on the back of an envelope: GONE WEST, TURKEYS IN CELLAR, THANKS. J. REESE, and propped the envelope on the table where she'd see it.

Stopping a moment in the yard, he sniffed at the icy breeze and wondered if the storm was really over or was it just waiting for a fool drifter to ride into it? Didn't make much difference, he thought, there's nothing left for you here.

Returning to the Calico Queen, Rose looked again at the horses standing at the hitch rail and made up her mind. Adjusting the cloth covering her basket, she thought, I might as well be hung for a sheep as a goat, and remembered the one about a bird in the hand is worth two in the bush as she pushed open the storm doors and went inside the dank room smelling of stale spilled beer, reeking tobacco smoke, old pine sawdust, and sour whiskey.

As the men at the bar turned to stare, she saw Colonel Wayne Damker with his hired hand at the end of the left side of the bar, and Fortunato Fajardo standing at the other end with his herder, while the banker, Max Gotch, stood in the center as if he were the boundary between the two opposed camps.

The men had shed their great coats and she noticed that the Colonel was wearing a six gun tied down to his right thigh. Fajardo wore an outfit of smooth dark colored material

---

that fit his long lean frame like a glove, but a pearl-handled six-gun hung snugly on his hip.

The banker appeared to be unarmed.

Behind the bar stood Dill Rafferty, wearing a striped shirt under a heavy brown vest. His two raw red hands rested palm down on the bar as he watched her approach.

Before he could tell her to scat, she innocently called out, "Cookies, anyone?" and pausing by a big potbellied stove, savored its warmth as she watched the men looking as if they all had been caught in a hen house after dark.

"I'm selling oatmeal cookies, Mr. Rafferty," she said. "I made them myself."

"We don't want any." Rafferty's voice broke as he cleared his throat. "Ladies ain't —"

"They're only two for a nickel, twelve for a quarter," she interrupted, staying by the stove.

"Lady, we're having a business discussion," Colonel Damker said.

"I'd say we all have some business problems of mutual concern," she replied.

"I'm concerned that your new hired hand set me afoot in the freezing cold this morning,' the Colonel turned to face her.

"On my range or yours?" Rose asked grimly.

"Some of the Bar D cattle were pushed through your fence by the blizzard. We were gathering them when your man came at us."

Damker's hired hand nodded, backing him up.

"You mean you didn't cut the fence again, Colonel?" Rose replied, her face reddening with anger.

"Of course he cut it!" came the soft, sibilant voice of Fortunato Fajardo.

"Maybe that's how my cattle disappeared last fall." Rose murmured, eyeing the Colonel intently.

"Lady, if you want a war, we'll be glad to give it to you!" the Colonel roared, "and as for the stinkin' sheepherder, he's so close to dyin', he ought to be prayin' instead of flappin' his big mouth!"

"I knew this would be a good day for me." Fajardo said, smiling.

"You gents ever think about your wives and children when you're on the prod?" Rose asked point blank.

"Please Mrs. Cameron," Max Gotch pleaded, "In your condition.... get on out of here—"

"Not until they answer my question," Rose said strongly.

Chapter Ten

Fortunato Fajardo, slim and lethal, stepped clear of the bar leaving Ignacio Ramirez, the herder to watch Shorty.

"De gran subida, gran caida" Fajardo murmured.

"That mean you quit?" Damker snarled.

"It means the bigger they are, the harder they fall. What are you waiting for big man?"

"Draw, you damned devil!" Damker yelled, his hand poised over the ivory butt of his six-gun.

KA-BOOM came the blast of a shotgun firing into the floor. The men froze a moment, then jerked around to stare at Rose holding the smoking short shotgun, her uncovered basket of cookies on the table.

"There must be a better way." Rose said, moving forward.

"Stay back!," Colonel Damker gritted, still ready to draw.

"I don't hold with settling differences with guns," Rose said, "and I'm not moving, not at least until I sell this basket full of cookies."

"I'll buy them all, Mrs. Cameron," Fortunato said, his glittering eyes fixed on the big cattleman. "Now, if you will please step aside—"

"Think of your baby, Mrs. Cameron," Max Gotch protested.

"You can stop them, Mr. Gotch." Rose turned to the banker. "Or do you hold mortgages on their land, too?"

Speechless, the banker stared at Rose.

"Verdad," Fortunato smiled. "He takes my sheep and range if I don't make the payments."

"How about you Colonel?" Rose asked.

"He holds a mortgage on the Bar D,..."

"Hearing you folks lamenting," the banker chuckled, regaining his composure, "reminds me of the dying rancher who named six bankers to be his pallbearers. He figured bankers had carried him so long they ought to finish the job."

"It's no joking matter, Mr. Gotch," Rose said, and turned to Damker and Fajardo, "Don't you see how he set you both onto me, then he sets you against each other?"

"This is between you and me, sheepman," Damker growled, sidestepping clear of Rose, the fingers of his right hand splayed out and working nervously.

"I don't back up, zorillo," Fajardo retorted. "I don't steal a widow's cattle either."

KER-CHUNK. Rose cocked the other hammer of the shotgun and swung the muzzle back and forth.

"Hold it, gents!" Rose said sharply. "She's loaded with double ought buck."

"Careful with that thing, lady." Damker said, wincing as the awesome muzzle pointed his way.

"Ni modo." Fortunato shrugged, stepped back and put both hands on top of the bar. "You have the voice of reason, Madam."

"You?" Rose demanded of the slope-shouldered cattle-man.

"For now," Damker sighed heavily, turning back to the bar. "Put that scatter-gun away before it goes off by itself."

"I'd say that's some progress," Rose said. "Now, Mr. Fajardo, what's your business problem?"

"I'm broke." Fortunato said quietly, shrugging his shoulders eloquently.

"How about you, Colonel?" Rose asked.

"I can't even pay Shorty." Damker replied, downcast.

"All of us are working for the bank." Rose nodded.

Fajardo, Damker and Rose stared at the banker in silent accusation.

"I am not to blame for a money panic in the East," Gotch snapped. "Be reasonable."

"Yet, it's true." Rose murmured. "The more we lose, the more you gain."

"At the very worst," Gotch said slowly, as if explaining an arithmetic problem to children, "the bank might have to foreclose, but I'd never drive my friends off their land."

"Then we'd all be your sharecroppers," Rose said

"There is an easy solution to our problem if you'd care to consider it." Gotch said smiling. "No one has to suffer if we work together.".

"Go on," Fortunato said suspiciously.

"Let us say that the bank takes over the Circle C and finds Mrs. Cameron a good job in town where she can send the boy to a good school."

"So you've got the Circle C. Then what?" Colonel Damker asked.

"Then we arrange to rent the bottom land to Mr. Fajardo for his sheep, and we also sell the water to your Bar D and rent you the western range."

"Why don't I just do that myself?" Rose asked, regaining her smile.

"You could sell out to me, Mrs. Cameron, and bypass the bank." Damker said.

"I'm not selling," Rose retorted, and taking her basket, backed away from the bar.

"Don't be upset, Mrs. Cameron," Fortunato said politely. "Suppose we make a partnership. We can hold the ranch together fifty fifty."

"And run sheep on it?"

"You would have your garden and your turkeys, and you wouldn't need to move out." Fortunato said, nodding.

"I didn't say she'd have to move out!" Damker exploded, "The buildings don't make a nevermind!"

"There's something else out there that's mighty important to me," Rose said, her eyes searching each face for a hint of human kindness.

"Name it," Damker rasped.

"My husband's grave," Rose said quietly, moving toward the door.

"I beg your pardon, madam," Fajardo apologized softly. "I should have known."

"Wait," Gotch said, "let's not be too hasty."

But Rose pushed past him and through the door to the boardwalk.

The cluttered street was all but deserted except for a tall stork-like man with a grey handlebar mustache approaching. He wore a long coat made of coyote pelts decorated by Indian beadwork, and pinned over his heart was a brass star.

"Howdy, Marshal," Rose smiled. "Care to buy some Christmas cookies?"

"I'd sure like to, but on my pay there ain't nothin' ever left over. What I want to know is have you got a new hand out at the ranch?"

She hesitated, wondering how he knew the stranger had stopped by, and why it was important.

"No, sir," she said. "I haven't hired anybody."

"Maybe just a visitor...?" he persisted.

"Marshal, there was a man came in just as the blizzard hit." she said, looking into his keen eyes.

"Have a name?" the Marshal asked gently.

"Reese. Joel Reese, as I recall."

"That's him all right," the Marshal nodded.

"Is he wanted?" Rose asked, wondering if she were in for another disappointment.

"No, not by the law anyway," the Marshal said. "His sidekick got himself killed robbin' the bank over at Spring Creek last summer, but Reese was cleared."

"Who's lookin' for him then?" she asked, remembering the somber face, the troubled eyes of the stranger in black, a face she'd liked and trusted on first sight.

"Seems he had words with both your neighbors," the Marshal said with a twinkle in his eyes. "They been curious about him."

"I'm worrying more about a war right on top of the Circle C," Rose said. "I don't want any killing over my ranch."

"Those are strong men and they follow their own ways," the Marshal said, "Good day to you, ma'am."

Rose turned numbly, walking slowly down the side street that would lead across the gulch.

Passing by the small, cobbled together cabins, she came to the corner building that seemed like such a haven to her now, even though only the night before she'd feared it as if it were an opium den.

Pushing through the door, she saw Ira talking to the pair of men in buckskin and sheepskin coats, drinking coffee.

"Hello, Rose," Ira smiled broadly. "How did your cookie sale go?"

"Folks are fat in the middle and poor at each end," she said, downcast.

"I'm sorry. Maybe tomorrow."

"Have a cookie with your coffee, gents," Rose said. "A present from me."

The men thanked her and looked questioningly at Ira.

"This is Rose Cameron. She's got a sick boy in the back room. Rose, remember Faren and Ralph from this morning? They been out north trapping for whatever they can catch."

"You know the Circle C out that way?" she asked the nearest man.

"Yes'm. We stopped by there. Nobody home."

"Did you see if the turkeys in the pen were alive?" she asked, trying to control her anxiety.

"What pen?" Ralph asked, mystified.

"Right alongside the house."

"Wasn't no turkeys nor even a pen near the house," Ralph said positively. "Was a bare patch there and some feathers... might have been a turkey pen once."

"No sign of a flock of turkeys?"

"We didn't poke around none, ma'am," Faren said. "but we'd have noticed a flock of turkeys for sure."

"For sure," Rose said tiredly and asked Ira, "How's Tommy?"

"Lena's still with him," Ira said, not answering her question.

"Excuse me," she said, hurrying back through the kitchen and down the hall to the small bedroom.

Lena sat in the chair by the bed, the boy's small hand in her own. Tommy's breath came raggedly as he slept; fever spots marked each cheek. His face was dry and hot to Rose's touch.

"The fever didn't go down any?" Rose whispered to Lena.

The red-haired girl shook her head, not looking into Rose's eyes.

"He's burning up," Rose touched Tommy's forehead and cast about in her mind for something she could do.

"I gave him some broth and kept him covered," Lena said apologetically, "but the fever only seems to get worse."

"It's so strange, Lena." Rose said, shaking her head, "It's nothing like croup or pneumonia or the ague...."

Coming back to the fork in the road, Nellie Damker halted her team and tried to sort out her opposing thoughts. To the left lay the town of Calico, going to the right would take her back to the Bar D.

She was acquainted with most of the business people in Calico but even though she'd known the town when it was just a crossroads, she still didn't feel involved in its rise or fall, because she was a country woman and the residents of Calico were townspeople.

At the ranch she felt secure, unafraid, confident that there was no task she couldn't handle, whether it be chopping the head off a rattler or castrating bull calves. It might be lonely a lot of the time, but it was home.

Still, she'd baked the spice cake and churned the butter and had it in her head that she would try to be friends with her neighbor.

The wind was picking up again. It might start blowing up more blizzard before dark.

Use your head, she told herself, go on back home and try it another day....

But that lady is in town right now and whatever help she has still won't be enough, and if you get caught by the storm, you can put up at the hotel....

"Gee!" she called to the team and jerked the reins. A moment later, Nellie Damker was on her way to Calico, hooting and laughing at her own madcap breakaway.

What would Wayne think if he could see her now? She laughed again at the image of his mustache bristling, his eyes blazing, his dour features set in an angry frown.

"Oh, he'd give you what for!" she chuckled, "but what the heck, he's mad at something all the time anyway, he might as well get serious about it...."

Anaberta Fajardo Ruiz had no thought of kinship with the town of Calico because other than buying supplies there, she had no connection. The church was not her church. The people were not her people. Few if any could speak her native tongue which had been spoken here long before the Anglos and their brutish language had arrived. Even their food was plain and unappetizing.

Why am I doing this? she wondered for the tenth time since she'd started the team off. For a friendless pregnant neighbor? No, surely she has more friends than I. She speaks their language, she probably fries steak and potatoes. She has Christmas this week instead of nine nights of posadas. She probably thinks Mexicans are intruders! She will fear you, thinking you have a blood-thirsty Aztec soul and want your land back. She will take you for a lowborn woman wanting a little wage for your help.

Ai, Dios! What am I doing? she worried.

I need to buy a few small presents for the children, she tried to excuse herself. After all, they should have their Christmas even though we have our problems. I will buy a few things and ask about the lady Mrs. Cameron, just to be sure she's well taken care of, and I may say a cautioning word to Fortunato if I happen to see him, then I will return promptly to my proper place before supper time. What is so crazy about that?

It is crazy because you are not telling the truth, she thought. You are worried about Fortunato because he put on the gun. You are worried about Mrs. Cameron because your conscience tells you that you have been a bad neighbor.

So what you must do is ask the storekeeper in perfect English how is the health of Mrs. Cameron, and then you must find Fortunato and make him come home with you, even if you have to cry and threaten him enough to melt his heart.

When he saw the stocky brown-faced lady come shyly in the door, George Veiten needed a moment to remember the sheepman's wife. She probably would have no money, he thought, and might even ask for credit, but at least she was a customer. Customers had become such rarities this past year that he stepped forward eager to please.

"Ja, senora," he greeted her, trying to speak the little shade-tree Spanish he'd learned on the border. "Guten dias."

For her part, Anaberta was determined to speak correctly the English she had tried to learn from her husband.

"Very good, I teenk is so," she said slowly. "Day."

"Kay 'uda?" Veiten beamed proudly.

"With easy," she said, making a polite smile.

"Komme a la estufa, und varmen zus manos," Veiten gestured to the hot potbellied stove.

"I am very kind, I teenk is so," Anaberta said, gaining more confidence.

"Jawohl, kay oder, bella riñon?" he asked, hoping riñon meant 'queen',

"You are very cold outside, I say he with my face wash and my pants down" she smiled warmly at the paunchy mercantiler, but wondering why he thought her kidney was beautiful.

"Yo sabo mucho," Veiten replied extra loudly, so she'd understand better. "Ja, es gut mucho."

"I wish to see a body of your husband," Anaberta said hesitantly.

"Es is mucho duro bei mir, ja," Veiten boomed.

"I think is more better my English now," Anaberta said, not understanding any of the deep guttural sounds roaring from the portly German. "Can yourself speak for he she, it?"

"Who?" Veiten asked, giving way to fear.

"They or them I teenk it is."

"Wait a minute, Missus," Veiten said, holding up both hands to stop the strange dialogue. "Something ain't right. What is it you want?"

"Mrs. Cameron?" Anaberta said, making it a question with the rise of her voice.

"Ja, ja, Mrs. Cameron. I don't know. But your husband, I know he's over at the bank." Veiten took Anaberta's elbow and escorted her to the door where he pointed out the brick building on the other corner.

"Bank?"

"Yes. Banco. Señor Fajardo went in there just a minute ago. You can't miss it."

"Mi esposo?" she asked, to be sure.

"Maybe. You go see," George Veiten said, opening the door for her and steering her out to the boardwalk.

"Thank you," Anaberta said, took Veiten's hand and leaned forward to kiss his cheek politely, then crossed the street.

By now she knew she'd gotten herself into a bigger problem than she'd expected because the wind was on the rise again and she'd never be able to get home before dark, and here she was in the midst of strangers who couldn't even understand English.

Yet if she could find her husband, he would help her.

Already she was forgetting the anger she'd felt when he walked out of the house wearing the gun.

Don't you forget, she warned herself. You tell him.

Even as she was hunched against the wind, crossing the street, Fortunato Fajardo was getting to his feet from the chair in front of Max Gotch's desk. Fajardo's face, calm and collected, did not reveal the terrible turmoil he felt filling his chest.

"So, if you can't, you can't," he said to the banker, still seated behind the desk.

"It is not me, Fortunato," Max Gotch said. "If I had my say about it, I'd declare a holiday and suspend all business transactions until it rains."

"A fiesta for the losers," Fortunato replied, forcing a smile.

"If it would just rain, or even snow hard, then we'd have something to bank on, but who knows? This country may look like a burned boot next summer."

"It has never been this bad before in the memory of my family," Fortunato said.

"But that won't wash with the auditors. I have to have some evidence that this country will still produce before the bank can extend any notes or loan out any more reserves."

"I'm not worried," Fortunato said, "my old mother has predicted heavy snow for this winter and bountiful rain in the summer."

"I sure hope she's right," Gotch said, getting to his feet, "but half the winter's gone by already and there's more dust than snow out there."

As the front door opened, both men saw the stocky Anaberta hurry inside and put her weight against the door to close it.

"Anaberta!" Fortunato said, surprised.

Turning to him she cried out in Spanish, "No lo mate!"

"Anaberta, my love," Fortunato, with an odd sense of joy that he'd not had before, replied in English "Why kill him?"

"Kill me?" Gotch raised his furry eyebrows.

"Pues quien?" she asked, coming directly to the two men. "Who then?"

"It is not your business, Anaberta," Fortunato said evasively. "What are you doing here?"

"I'm here to say what I came here to say," she said in a dramatic rush. "I take the gun!"

Gotch's head swiveled back and forth as he tried to make sense of the rapid conversation in an unfamiliar language.

He thought he understood the woman to say she intended to kill him, and in a way he could see that she might be justified, but on the other hand he couldn't believe that anyone in this valley could know all of the bank's private business.

When Anaberta defiantly tried to grab the pistol from Fortunato's holster, Gotch paled and in stepping backward, stumbled and fell to one knee.

Raising his hands in supplication, he cried out, "No! Don't do it!"

His outburst was unnecessary because Fortunato's hand was ahead of his wife's and covered the Colt's grip.

"This is crazy," Fortunato said to Gotch, then spoke in Spanish to his wife, "Little sweetheart, because you are so dear to me, I am taking you seriously. Now what is it you want?"

"I want to say that if you do not give me that gun, you must therefore sleep with the sheep!" she said passionately.

"You came all the way through a storm to tell me that?" Fortunato frowned in disbelief.

"What is it?" Gotch asked, rising and lowering his hands. "What is she saying?"

"She says I must sleep with the sheep!" Fortunato exploded with laughter. "And I was afraid the house had burned down!"

"That's a pretty good joke all right..." Gotch made a sick smile, "but what about the gun?"

"Yes, the gun," Fortunate said grimly. "What can a man do if his wife risks her life for him?"

"Just be agreeable," Gotch said shakily. "Don't cross her."

"Very well, my beautiful little wife," Fortunato said to Anaberta softly, "I'm going to give you a Christmas present."

Drawing the sleek revolver, Fortunato twirled the cylinder, removed the cartridges and handed her the empty pistol.

"Muchas gracias, heart of my heart," Anaberta said, slipping the gun into her goatskin bag. "You are a man among men."

"Not many women would come so far to see that their husbands were safe from harm," Fortunato said proudly.

"I came to help Mrs. Cameron, too," Anaberta said, looking at the floor.

"I heard she is staying across the gulch," Fortunato said, his pride deflated, "but first we must find shelter. This storm is not a plaything."

"I am your obedient woman," Anaberta said with a twinkle in her eye. "A sus ordenes."

"Well... it's like the one cardsharp said to the other cardsharp, 'If I can give you a hand, just let me know'," Gotch said, laughing heartily at his own joke.

Joel Reese had lost track of the days and dates during the sunless weather. It was close to Christmas, maybe even past, but with no family to spend the holiday with, no presents to give or receive, it didn't make much difference one way or the other.

A loner doesn't have much use for Christmas, he thought. It sets him apart from regular folks in the middle of winter just when everyone needs some cheering up.

Somebody ought to figure out a special rodeo or fiesta, hoo-raw, or baile... something extra for single riders in the big lonesome.

Riding the black stud southwesterly, he kept to the worn immigrant trail and after crossing a low range of mountains found the weather worsening and the temperature dropping.

Couldn't do much about it, anyway. The stud was as good a bottomed horse as there was, and he'd give all he could, but there were limits as to what you could ask from a horse, unless you decided the matter was so important you had to ask his life for it. Boardinghouse company in Carson at Christmas time though wasn't near that important.

Down home before the war, mama always tried to make a Christmas for the family, but there was so goshdarned little on the ranch they were glad to have her own special plum pudding and a couple roasted wild turkeys for dinner.

All the presents were handmade. Usually she gave out knitted socks and dad would give iron work from the black-smith shop. Anselmo gave rawhide braided quirts and fancy horse mane ropes and such. The others gave out whatever they could. There was no Christmas tree, just the big mantle over the fireplace where mama would put a spray of red ninebark berries and a couple of beeswax candles. At giving time they just handed out their unwrapped gifts a little shyly and received them in the same way. The plum pudding was the big thing, he smiled, thinking about it.

No tree, no Santa Claus, no fancy ribbons or wrappings, and still it'd be a grand time, just sharing out the best you could.

Late in the afternoon Reese rode into the yard of a trading post built mostly of adobe and lumber scavenged from abandoned Fort Churchill near by. Over its low doorway was nailed a crudely lettered sign: Buckland Station.

Hurrying out of the weather, Reese pushed through the door without knocking. Inside, once his eyes adjusted to the gloomy shadows, he saw the crude layout of makeshift counters holding general merchandise, barrels of flour and cornmeal, and sacks of grain stacked in a dark corner. Hams, strings of smoked sausages and sides of bacon hung from cobwebbed pole rafters.

"Sam Buckland at your service," a white bearded man rose from a stool by the potbellied stove to greet him, "What do you need?"

"Half a side of bacon," Joel said, "and maybe some bread."

"I got Squaw bread," the old trader said neutrally.

"That'll do," Reese said, "and add in about ten pounds of oats for my horse."

"Wind is on the rise again," Buckland said as he fetched a side of bacon down from its hook and cut it in two with a big butcher knife, "You going far?"

"Carson," Reese said.

"You can't make Carson before dark," Buckland said, "Better you stay here until this killer storm blows itself out."

"Can't." Reese said, paying the old trader. "There's not much time."

"You one of them time-crazy folks?" Buckland grinned. "I seen a lot of money-crazy folks that can't think of nothing but profit and savings while their lives go by, but not so many time-crazies chasin' the sun while their lives go by.

"Normal times I just work and mind my own business while my life goes by," Reese smiled, realizing the old trader was lonely and wanted to talk. "Any normal-time work over this way?"

"Been too dry," the trader shook his head, "No work any kind of crazy time. Ain't none in Carson either, but there'll be plenty of snow."

"Much obliged, Mr. Buckland," Reese said, and carried his supplies out to the black stud, filled his saddlebags and headed into the stiffening wind.

Needle sharp sleet pecked at his face until without slowing the black, he pulled his muffler up and his hat brim down and leaned forward over the horse's neck like a knight in shaggy armor tilting against the dragon wind.

The immigrant trail, rutted deep in the ground, was easy enough to follow despite the storm, but when the pale sun lowered behind the gigantic Sierras, Joel was forced to turn off into a grove of cottonwoods alongside the Carson River.

As the last of the light failed, he found a small haven protected from the rising wind, built his fire of cottonwood twigs, and fed the black horse half the bag of oats.

The storm was too vicious to dawdle about the fire, and after a sandwich of hot bacon and the heavy unleavened bread, he crawled into his soogan.

Carson wasn't far, he thought tiredly, no more'n three or four hours depending on how much snow fell in the night.

Yet what was the hurry? No one expected him. No one was waiting. Maybe old Sam Buckland had the right idea.

Some folks wasted their lives being money-crazy, others wasted their lives being time-crazy, and others did both.

Still, he was down to his last thirty dollars. He had to find work or starve, and he reckoned he'd stick up a stage or a bank before he just gave up on everything, especially living.

All around his sheltered camp, the wind played the tall trees like harp strings, hammering out primitive chords, rising and falling in a cadence of chaos, and as the snow came gusting through the night, Reese thought it sounded like a crazed prophet preaching death and resurrection. It wasn't screaming words like repent or atone or forgive, though. It sounded more like 'Change your ways.... do something different.... wrong is a rut, right is a revelation...,' but none of it made sense.

Half asleep, he saw Jeff's sun scoured face grinning at him, and he murmured brokenly, 'I'm sorry Jeff, I should have guessed you'd play a dumb trick like that. Should have known and should have stopped you....'

The once cheery face darkened with anger and Reese heard the wind's scourging voices howling through the trees, 'change your ways.... do something different.... wrong is a rut, right a revelation....' and he wondered if that commanding chorus was connected to Jeff's unhappy visage.... 'change, change your ways.... live, live now, live now all, live life!.... Live all life.... life, revelation, and resurrection....'

I don't understand.... he thought, feeling a heavy ache of remorse in his chest; I let you down.... can't make up for it.... and I don't know how to change....

Now Jeff was screaming at him in a fury, desperately trying to tell him something, but it wouldn't translate into good sense, and he woke himself up crying out in agony, "No!"

Stubbornly, he tried to tell himself that he was tormented because he was guilty, and this nightmare like all the others, was just punishment.

At first light, he searched vainly through the fresh snow for more dry twigs but it was impossible to build a quick cooking fire and at the rate the snow was blowing off the mountains, his most prudent judgment was to hurry into Carson first and eat later.

As he mounted up, he remembered the nightmare. Nothing had changed. The wind still gusted from the northwest, the hard snow flakes mixed with sleet still peppered his face, and yet he felt something was different.

As he pushed on against the wind, he thought he was still Joel Reese looking for honest work, and that was his life., He was always either working or looking for work to keep himself alive. It had been that way ever since the end of the war. The only event that had disturbed the pattern was Jeff sneaking off to rob a bank with an empty gun.

The good black stallion broke the trail through the hard crusted snow as they stayed close to the river.

The footing became more difficult and the black horse was tiring while the storm seemed to be increasing in ferocity.

"We get into Carson, we'll hole up for awhile and try to hang onto our money till we turn up a job." Joel muttered encouragement to the black horse.

Lord, he almost groaned aloud, it might not be till spring the way everybody was hanging on to their money. Four months maybe. Four months on thirty dollars would make it less'n eight dollars a month. Can't be done. Can't keep myself on eight dollars a month, nor you either.

Could he sell the horse just to stay alive till spring?

"Nope, don't worry Coalie, we're going down to ruin to-gether," he said wryly.

As the black bowed his neck against the wind, Reese huddled inside his great buffalo robe and without trying, saw the hopelessness of his situation. Even if he could find work at Carson it would lead from nowhere to nothing, like a trail you follow along that grows smaller and smaller until it just runs up a tree....

Got to be something better'n that, he thought as the freezing wind buffeted him and the horse, but what? Your trade is riding, your tools are your rope and saddle. Yet now with the drought there's more riders than cows....

You could turn around and help that widow woman back in Calico... but she can't pay wages either.... What about the boy?

You could do something for nothing for a change, he thought, frowning. You couldn't be much worse off....

You could change. You could do something different. You could get out of the rut and you might think up a new idea....

With the wind and snow obscuring his vision, he let the black pick his way alongside the river, and he visualized how the long, long trail ahead forked in three ways and pointing down each fork was a freshly painted signboard. The one on the left said Young Rider Wanted. The middle one said Easy Bank Stick-up and the third one had only a big question mark....

That's a change, Reese thought. I'll take it.

But where does it go? he asked himself, remembering the dream of Jeff's furiously crying out to him.

It goes out of the rut, he thought, and forgetting Jeff, he remembered Rose Cameron and her feverish little boy, a boy wanting his own saddle.

It don't end there and it don't end here, he thought and smiled.

Passing occasional wagons and buckboards on the wagon road, he felt a new confidence and sense of purpose, and the black picked up his pace, lifted his head and looked more like a proud horse passing the others by.

It took awhile to find the saddle shop because it was a strange town to Reese and he had to ask a couple of times before he found the long, low building down by the river.

A sign over the door said: DURBY SADDLES.

Off to the side the river had been flumed over to a slowly turning water wheel, its axle extended into the building.

Going inside, he saw work benches, wooden vises, an old, heavy duty sewing machine, and a great wooden tanning drum turning from the power of the water wheel outside.

Half a dozen new saddles rode a long wooden rack, their leather dry and clean, some stamped, some not, each one different.

He heard hides tumbling in the big wooden drum, becoming a little more pliable with every revolution.

A middle-aged man of medium size came forward to meet Reese. Over his straight brown hair he wore a big brown Stetson hat, and an untrimmed mustache half covered his generous mouth.

"Howdy.'

"You Asa Durby?"

"I am."

"I need a boy's saddle. Spanish American tree. Swell fork, low cantle. Sam Stagg double rig. Seat should be about two hands across."

The saddlemaker frowned, and asked "Boy's saddle? You know the boy?"

"From over by Calico," Reese said. "Can you make that up right away?"

Looking up at the tall man in black, Durby shook his head and smiled, "No, I can't make it up right away. I'm behind on my orders, but I think I can help you out."

Leading Reese to the end of the long room, he rummaged among shelves of bridles, cinches, martingales, and brought out a brand new miniature saddle.

"I dunno...." Reese shook his head doubtfully. "It's special for a boy who knows what he wants."

"I got an order from Calico way last spring, along with five dollars earnest money." Durby said, "Maybe the boy's dad copied off the order and sent it in. Anyway, it's the exact same thing, except he wanted a plate of engraved silver riveted to the back of the cantle."

Durby lifted the small saddle to the light and Reese saw the silver plate engraved: For Tommy, top © rider, with love, Dad.

By the time Nellie Damker drove down the main street, the temperature had dropped and the wind was rising again, although it brought no measurable snow.

She observed the littered, ratty street with disgust and casting a look at the westering sun, realized it was already too late to return to the ranch in daylight, and when she saw her husband's and Shorty's horses at the hitchrail, she pulled the team to a halt in front of the Plaza Hotel.

Inside she found Ophelia Masson knitting a grey and white shawl in the ante room.

"Afternoon, Mrs. Masson," Nellie called out, and deciding to let Shorty look out for himself, said, "I'd like a room for two for tonight, please."

"Let's see—you're..." Ophelia said, trying to remember the name to match the familiar wizened apple face.

"Nellie Damker, Bar D," Nellie said, exasperated. "I been tradin' in this town before ever there was a dream of a hotel and still nobody knows my name."

"It's the weather, Mrs. Damker," Ophelia said, pinching her lips together, irritated with herself for daydreaming about a little baby instead of paying attention to business. "That'll be a dollar in advance."

As Nellie laid a silver dollar on the counter, she asked, "have you seen anything of Rose Cameron?"

"As a matter of fact," Ophelia Masson said, "she was selling cookies out here on the corner an hour ago."

"Sellin' cookies! I thought she was nine months pregnant—"

"She is," Ophelia said carefully, "but she has no... um... resources...."

"She here?" Nellie asked, perplexed.

"No, no, she's staying over across the gulch someplace," Ophelia said, looking at the floor.

"Well, if that ain't a hell of a note!" Nellie snapped, understanding most if not all of the picture now.

Ophelia Masson was too shocked by the plain language to reply, and Nellie went outside, fuming.

She drove on to the livery barn at the end of the street, and put the team in Elroy Morrison's care.

"Don't you worry about a thing, ma'am," Morrison mumbled, trying to get his fuzzy thoughts together. "You can count on me."

"I'm not sure," Nellie Damker said sharply, and ignoring the loopy-legged livery man's vague protests, went to the feed bin and fed her horses herself.

"Now you don't need to do nothing except keep your jug warm," Nellie said as she went out the door.

"Damn woman's got hair on her chest," Morrison grumbled to himself, wondering how she knew about the jug.

Nellie braced herself against the cold and leaned against the wind as she made her way down the trashy boardwalk to the Mercantile.

Inside, she went directly to the stove and warmed her hands while George Veiten got up from his checker game and asked, "What can I do for you, Mrs. Damker?"

"Well, at least you know my name," the small, feisty lady fired back at him. "You got a boy around here can fetch my husband?"

"Yes, ma'am," Veiten said and called back into the shadows. "Martin—go get Mr. Damker from the—wherever he is,"

"Yes, papa," Martin replied and ran out the door for the dash across the street without putting on his coat.

"Can't you even say the word saloon?" Nellie barked at him. "Hell, it's no sin for a man to go to a saloon, at least not yet."

"There was some shootin' over there," Veiten stammered.

"My husband?" she frowned.

"Nobody's hurt yet." Veiten said nervously. "You need something else?"

"Not just now," Nellie said. "Do you know where Rose Cameron is staying?"

"Rose? Rose Cameron—" Veiten murmured as if the names were puzzles in his memory.

"Damn it, George!" Nellie snapped at him.

"Yes, Rose Cameron... she's over on the other side of the gulch last I heard."

"Where exactly?" Nellie demanded.

"Well... there's a barn, you know, that an old bum fixed up for that kind of people, if you know what I mean...." George Veiten's voice faltered. "She's helpin' out over there."

"Helping out! My stars in heaven, why isn't somebody helpin' her out!" Nellie managed to keep her voice down to an irate squawk.

"Well, you know, we all want to help..." Veiten's face flushed as he looked at the floor, "but she's mighty independent, you know, and don't have no money...."

The opening door stopped her retort for which George Veiten was profoundly grateful.

"What are you doing here, woman?" boomed the commanding voice of the Colonel.

"What's this about a shootin'?" Nellie countered strongly.

"It wasn't anything. Just that fool woman from the Circle C with her sawed off greener," the Colonel said, softening his gruff bravado.

"Who was you goin' to shoot with?" Nellie hung on like a terrier.

"That sheepherder..." Damker said plainly, "accusing me of rustling, trying to get the ranch away from her."

"I heard that sheepherder is slick as wool fat with a gun," Nellie said. "Likely you owe your life to that lady."

"I'da blowed him up like a duck in a rain barrel," the Colonel said, his voice on the rise.

"You with the arthritis locking up every joint in your body?" Nellie said, shaking her head. "I'm not sayin' you aren't brave enough, I'm just sayin' that lady done us both a big favor."

"Maybe," the Colonel said, holding on to his pride, "but I'm not about to back down from anybody."

"Listen, husband," Nellie said quietly, "it's time you started thinking about me. If I lose you, what have I got? A headboard on a sorry hill? Mister, you better listen to me. You start to playin' mister big man with the gun, I'm goin' west on the next stage."

"You wouldn't!" Damker stared at her.

"You ever known me to lie in all this time?"

"No, Nellie," the Colonel murmured, torn between de-manding obedience and begging her to relent.

"Make up your mind, Colonel. I won't chew my cabbage twice," Nellie said.

"Take care of this, Mr. Veiten," the Colonel said, un-buckling the old gunbelt. "I surrender."

Chapter Eleven

*T*he two shawl-cowled women bowed like mothering wings over the bed where Tommy fitfully slept and kept their silent vigil as the boy struggled for breath, until at length Lena shook her head and murmured, "He's not worse, but he's not much better. That's against us because day by day he's wearing out."

"What more can we do?" Rose asked quietly, deep gray smudges under her eyes.

"I want you to lie down alongside him and get some rest."

"I'm not that tired," Rose protested, sitting on the side of the bed, and touching Tommy's cheek, she added, "He's hotter'n a pistol."

"It's some kind of pernicious poisoning," Lena said.

"Too many things comin' at me," Rose said tiredly. "Ever have that problem, Lena?"

"Once. When I was fifteen."

"Where was that?"

"Illinois. Farmersville. Little town no better'n this one."

"That's sayin' something!" Rose frowned. "A man likely...."

"Sure. Only he was just a boy and purty as a little red wagon, and I played the fool for him. Came reckonin' time, his mama sent him back east to school. The whole town closed up against me. My daddy had been a teller in the bank

for twenty-six years, and he was just one push from bein'
fired.

"Mama came home red-eyed every time she went to buy
groceries. A mean town."

"The baby?"

"A little boy, fat and jolly. I named him Lancelot and
called him Lance," Lena said softly, remembering. "The day
he was born, the whole town put on their funeral clothes,
hitched up their black buggies, and made a parade down the
street by our house, never sayin' anything, just settin' in their
buggies looking straight ahead, goin' at a slow walk, all in
black, passin' by like they was leavin' the graveyard and I was
the one being buried."

"Poor child!" Rose felt a wave of compassion rise in her
breast.

"Then they all said I had to give him up, put him in an
orphanage. Said I wasn't a fit mother. Got my daddy and
mama to houndin' me, too, so's I couldn't think straight. I
took the money in the sugar bowl one night and run off with
Lance. Then I found out the rest of the world was not much
different'n Farmersville."

"The baby?"

"Finally had to give him up," Lena murmured. "I made
sure he went to a good home. He'll get an education and I
know where he is."

"What a pity," Rose said, reaching over and taking
Lena's slender hand.

"Sometimes I surely miss him hard," Lena said, her voice
cracking.

"Someday.... someday...." Rose said, squeezing her hand.

"That's what I go by, Rose. Someday...."

Joel halted the black stud on the hill above the ranchstead. The small saddle, sacked in burlap, rode securely from
his saddle horn. Letting the stud take a breather, Joel looked
down at the winding creek, the barren cottonwoods, and sycamores, the empty buildings.

There it is, he thought, every man's dream. All it needs
is a family wanting to care for it, but they're gone and the
place is dead as a fried mule.... Cool water in the summer,
bottom land hay for the winter. A man could plant pines and
junipers along the fence lines to soften the wind and a
woman could grow a wagon load of tomatoes and cabbages
there next to the creek. Keep a tame cow for milk, a couple
pigs and some steers for meat, then sell off a well-mannered
saddle horse whenever you needed a little cash money.... It
doesn't seem like it'd be so terrible hard but I reckon you'd
need good neighbors first of all....

Sitting on the bed alongside Tommy, Rose Cameron
held his small hand in her own as he lay staring up at the
ceiling without speaking. She felt the wind hammering at the
walls, and wondered if the whole country wasn't ready to
blow away.

If we could just get a good deep snow pack that'd fill the
streams and get the grass growing in the spring, she thought,
but so far it seemed all they were going to get was a few crystals of wind whipped ice that would do little toward holding
the topsoil together.

A quick knock on the door brought her thoughts back to
the present, and she muttered, "Now what?"

The door opened and Ira stuck his head in to announce,
"Got a visitor, Rose."

Now filling the lower part of the doorway, she saw a woman she'd seen in the Mercantile in times past but whose visit was a complete surprise.

"Mrs. Damker," Rose murmured, rising from the bed.

"Don't get up, Rose," the older lady said, "and call me Nellie, please."

"Sit down—Nellie," Rose said, wondering what the woman wanted, but gesturing at a wooden chair near the bed.

"Rose...." Nellie said, placing the cloth covered cake pan and the butter pail at the foot of the bed, "Rose... I thought maybe you'd like a little treat."

"That's mighty kind of you, Nellie," Rose said, still wary.

"I went over to your ranch, but there was no one there, so I figured you must've come to town."

"I couldn't keep Tommy out there in the norther," Rose said.

"Poor boy," Nellie said, touching Tommy's forehead. "Has he had the fever long?"

"It comes and goes," Rose said.

"Have you tried Feverfew tea?"

"Yes, and Golden Seal and Echinacea, too," Rose said. "Nothing seems to work."

"Then it's deep in the blood."

"It's not blood poisoning," Rose said. "Doc Snarph would have figured that out."

"And the baby?" Nellie asked.

"Any time." Rose smiled.

"I wonder if maybe you need some help, I could stay close by," Nellie offered.

"No offense, Nellie," Rose said, straight forwardly, "after all this time, what's changed your mind?"

"The truth of it is, I'm ashamed of myself for not coming sooner," Nellie said grimly.

"That goes both ways," Rose said, "but we can't help it if we live so far apart and there's always the work."

"I decided yesterday I could do anything if I just made the effort, and now I'm glad I've done it," Nellie said. "There's no law says we have to live out our lives slaving away like damn outcasts."

"Your children are all gone?" Rose asked.

"Years ago," Nellie nodded.

"It's a hard life," Rose said sympathetically, "and it doesn't seem to get any easier."

"That's the truth," Nellie nodded, "but I been thinkin' it doesn't have to be lonesome, too. My house is no more'n six miles from your house. Even counting the jog in the road, it's still only an hour or two ride."

"I don't know as it makes much difference now, Nellie," Rose said, but she noticed Tommy staring at her, and changed the direction of her words in mid sentence, "that is, until Tommy gets back on his feet."

"I think I understand," Nellie said, "but that won't be long."

"When I was a girl back in Decorah, my mother and her friends used to get together and make quilts every Thursday afternoon at one or the other of their houses," Rose said, remembering. "I recall everyone had a good time and they made some quilts besides."

"I passed through Decorah years and years ago," Nellie said, smiling. "It was a pretty town, all green with lots of trees and a river winding through it."

"Why did we ever come out here?" Rose asked, chuckling.

"I guess 'cause the men asked us to," Nellie said. "I sure wouldn't have ever done it on my own."

"Yes, but when you're young, you need challenges," Rose said, "and everything is fun at first."

"I guess I better move along, Rose," Nellie said, creakily getting to her feet. "I just wanted to come and tell you six miles is nothing amongst friends."

"Oh, Nellie," Rose said, close to weeping, "I do want us to be friends. It's been so—"

"I know just what you're feelin', Rose," Nellie said, putting her arm around Rose's shoulders. "You don't need to tell me."

A rap on the door broke the moment. A second later, Lena poked her head in and with a big smile announced, "Another visitor, Rose. You're gettin' to be as popular as a two-headed calf."

Coming in the door, stocky, energetic Anaberta Fajardo Ruiz stopped suddenly, seeing the two women together.

Looking timidly from Rose to Nellie, she started to back up, but Fortunato appeared behind her, and said quickly, "Ladies, may I present my wife, Anaberta. She has little English, but she speaks to you from the heart of a woman."

"I you bring regalo... baby..." Anaberta said slowly, looking at Rose.

"First, Anaberta, I'm pleased to know you and I want you to meet our other neighbor, Nellie Damker," Rose said, smiling.

Fortunato quickly translated, and impulsively Anaberta went to Rose, wrapped her arms around her bulk and kissed her on the cheek. Turning to Nellie, she extended both hands and said, "Con mucho gusto conocerle!"

"Well! I'll be damned!" Nellie exclaimed, grinning, "It's about time!"

Rummaging in her large handbag, Anaberta brought out a parcel wrapped in newspaper and gave it to Rose amidst a hurried burst of Spanish, which Fortunato translated, "It is a gift of love from her to you and she is sorry she was unable to come sooner."

As Rose undid the wrapping, Anaberta said proudly to Nellie, "I make...."

Rose unfolded a soft lambs wool baby's blanket carefully woven to gain the most warmth, and sectioned into a pattern of blue and pink squares.

"It's beautiful," Rose, said, overwhelmed by the richness of the gift.

Anaberta put her finger on a pink square and said, "Rosa, niño," and moving her finger again, she said, "Azul, niña."

"Heck, I can understand that," Nellie grinned. "It's kind of dual purpose, depending on whether we get a boy or a girl."

"How many children do you have?" Rose asked.

Anaberta's response was another burst of rapid Spanish along with waving four open fingers and patting her abdomen like a busy semaphore.

"We have four children," Fortunato said, "and are expecting another in a few months. They are three boys and a girl now, the oldest is five."

"That's an armload," Rose said to the proud Anaberta, smiling.

Turning to Fortunato she asked, "I'm already beginning to understand the language better. How do you say 'slow down'?"

"Mas despacio—por favor," he replied.

Rose turned back to Anaberta and repeated, "Mas despacio. Anaberta— por favor."

"Sure," Anaberta said, smiling. "Talk slow."

"You see?" Rose said. "We get along just fine."

"We were talking about making quilts," Nellie said, lifting the luxuriant blanket. "Maybe Anaberta would join us."

As Fortunato translated the invitation, Tommy said weakly, "Mama...."

"Yes, Tommy," Rose said turning her attention to the boy.

"The ranch," Tommy murmured weakly. "I mean, are we going to lose it?"

Sound asleep Rose Cameron dreamed she was lost in a deep mine inside a mountain and was feeling her way cautiously toward a distant pinpoint of light when a strange, unknown animal leaped on her back and sank its teeth into her shoulder.

Struggling against the iron grip of the animal, she started to cry out defiantly, when she felt a slim hand touch her cheek and heard Lena's voice in her ear, whispering, "Time to wake up, Rose."

Rose opened her eyes, trying to remember where she was, then realized it was morning, day before Christmas morning.

Nodding to Lena, she reached over and touched Tommy's still burning forehead, then slipped out of the bed.

"I'm sorry—you were dreaming...." Lena said, looking intently at Rose.

"Bad, too," Rose said, rubbing her face with both big hands. "Time to go to work?"

"No, it's not that. It's that banker man Gotch. He's all in a lather. Wants to see you in his office, he says soon as possible," Lena smiled.

"What in the world—?" Rose said, wondering why Max Gotch would have any urgent business with her. "I've still got a few days...."

Rose took a moment to scrub her face and pat out the wrinkles in her dress before putting on her coat and scarf and mittens.

"I'll be right back," she sang out to Ira as she went through the kitchen to the front door.

"You go slow, hear?" Ira called after her.

Feeling the bite of the freezing cold on her cheeks, Rose bumbled across the gulch to main street and went down the one block to the red brick bank building.

The teller with the green shade hiding his eyes, avoided her glance and didn't respond to her greeting, as she walked heavily toward the rear of the narrow room.

"Ah, good morning, Mrs. Cameron." Gotch turned his chair around to face her as she sank into the other chair. "I was just thinking that Noah would have been a great financier because he floated so many partnerships when the whole world was in liquidation!"

"You didn't ask me over here to tell jokes," she said.

"I'm concerned about a range war," Gotch said seriously. "unless we do something to stop it."

"I'm out of it," Rose said, "No one will listen to me."

"We'd best be practical," Gotch said, making a steeple of his fingers and setting it under his pointed chin.

"Can you give me an extension?"

"Always remember, Mrs. Cameron, something is better than nothing," Gotch said softly, avoiding the question, "Suppose I were to offer you the position of caretaker at the Circle C in exchange for a quit claim deed. I would also give your children the same benefits as my own—clothing, education, medical care...."

"If that drifter hadn't burned up my turkey pen—," Rose murmured, "I might have made it through."

"Let me give you a hundred dollars cash to tide you over." Gotch said sympathetically.

Rose thought of Tommy lying in bed, gasping for breath, and tried to picture him fifteen years from now. Tall and ruggedly handsome like his father, but what else? Would he be just a drifting cowhand unable to read or write, or might he grow up to be money wise and secure, perhaps working his way to the presidency of this very bank?

And the unborn babe, what chance in this world would it have?

"Do I understand my job would be just taking care of the place, nothing on the sly?" Rose asked, blushing but speaking out.

"Mrs. Cameron, I'm a businessman, nothing else. I have no such designs, believe me," he said flatly, and brought out a document with the blank places all filled in with a tight Spencerian script, and passed it over to her.

"Sign this and you'll avert a useless range war and gain a secure future for yourself and your loved ones," he murmured.

"An education for my children?"

"Clear through Yale if they want."

"Jim wanted me to hold on," she said doubtfully. "I promised."

"Your husband wanted your son to have a fair chance in life," Gotch said. "I'm guaranteeing that."

Again Rose thought of Lena's being pressured into the hard choice of sacrificing what she loved most for her boy's best interest.

It's a hard world, she thought without bitterness, and a mother alone in it doesn't have a chance.

Dipping a pen into the inkwell, Gotch extended it to her, and said smoothly, "Just sign there at the bottom and all your worries are over."

Leaning forward over the desk, she sighed and carefully wrote her name on the document, and the banker touched his green blotter to the signature, slipped the paper into a desk drawer, took five twenty dollar gold pieces from a leather pouch and put them in her hand.

As she got to her feet, the front door burst open and Joel Reese, big and threatening in his great coat filled the doorway with a worried look on his face until he saw her standing back in the shadowed room.

"Mrs. Cameron… " he said, relief in his voice, "I been lookin' all over…."

"Who?" Gotch stared at the big man.

"Joel Reese!" Rose said angrily, "Whatever….?"

"I got to thinkin'…." Reese stammered. "The land… the horses… the boy—"

"Worry no more, my friend, the Circle C ranch is now mine," Gotch smiled.

Joel's face revealed a moment of sudden pain as if he'd been lashed by a rawhide quirt, but his voice held steady. "That right, ma'am?"

"That's right," Rose sputtered angrily. "You been roughing up my neighbors, burning my turkey pen, feeding the coyotes...."

"I pushed those Bar D cattle back where they belonged, and the woolies, too," Joel tried to explain.

"What you should have done was taken care of my turkeys!" Rose stormed. "They were my last chance and you just turned 'em out and burned up their pen, so's you could stay warm and cozy!"

"Ma'am...." Joel tried again.

"It's all over," Rose cut him off. "Get on out of here, you, you... drifter!"

"Weary, stubble faced, and hungry, Joel Reese nodded and said politely, "Yes'm."

Chapter Twelve

*C*lose to tears, Rose Cameron kept her face averted as she trudged back to Ira's Bar 'n Grill.

"You all right, Rose?" Ira called out as she came in the door, seeing the tear stains and the bowing of her shoulders.

"It's over," she said dully. "I sold out to the bank."

"I'm sorry," Ira said.

"It's all for the best," she shook her head.

Passing through the kitchen and down the hall to the room, Rose found Lena trying to feed Tommy some hot broth. His dull eyes brightened when he saw his mother.

"You're doing better, Tommy."

"I guess," he spoke hoarsely. "I just ache all over."

Rose let her bulk gently down on the side of the bed and touched his forehead.

"You'll be right as rain tomorrow." She said, forcing a cheerful smile.

"It's better out home," he said weakly.

"We got to get you well first, Tommy," Rose said, feeling like weeping again. "Get you well and goin' to school."

"I just want to ride around our ranch like Dad," Tommy said, closing his eyes.

Grimly Joel Reese tethered the black stud to the hitchrail in front of the Calico Queen and looked up and down the almost empty street, its litter of broken boxes, demolished kegs, empty tins, and bottles and piles of horse manure mercifully covered by a thin sheeting of sooty snow.

A big gray rat chased a smaller one from under the boardwalk across the street and off toward the low rise of Boot Hill.

Likely they'd figured that hill was the worst property in town when they were looking for a place to start a graveyard, Reese thought.

He gazed up at that rough brushy knoll with tilted headboards outlined against the sullen sky, and saw a pair of burros pawing the ground, looking for a wisp of grass.

There it was. The end. The closed door. The final destination of every man's trip through life. Yet the mean little town chose not to look at it, nor take care of it, as if to say, 'the dead don't care'.

'Course the dead don't care, Joel thought, but it is the living that suffer deep down for their neglect.

Entering the dark, dank saloon, he strode up to the bar and said to Dill Rafferty, "Good morning. A little brandy, please."

Rafferty put a small glass in front of the tall man and brought out a bottle. "Say when."

"When it's full," Reese said.

"Mighty early in the day," Dill Rafferty said, pouring to the brim. "That'll be ten cents."

Reese laid a dime on the bar, picked up the glass and looked around the empty room. "Too early for business?" he asked

"Whole town's dead," Dill said somberly. "I'll be out of here by spring...."

"Can't change it?" Reese asked, lifting the glass.

"Better to start all over again fresh," Dill said gloomily, mopping the bar with a grey wet rag.

Reese finished off the glass, nodded to Dill, and said, "We got to do different, get out of the rut."

Squaring his shoulders, Joel turned and went out the door into the street.

Whacking his hands together to rid the chill, he climbed the steps to the bank, stomped the muck off his boots and opened the door.

At the far end of the narrow room, Max Gotch sat at his desk, studying a document and making notes in a green cloth covered ledger.

The banker's head bobbed with approval. Leaning back, he rubbed his soft hands together as if he were shaking hands and congratulating himself, until he saw the man in black.

"Well, look what the cat drug in," Gotch smiled. "Good morning, sir, what can I do for you?".

"I mean to take you for a little walk," Reese said quietly. "I want to show you this miserable town."

"I don't need to see this town, mister," Gotch smiled. "I own most of it."

"Maybe that's the problem," Reese said. "Get your coat on."

"I'm going nowhere with you," the banker's eyes bulged anxiously.

"I don't want your money, Mr. Gotch," Reese said, "I just want to have your company for a spell."

The banker's eyes dropped from the smoldering auger in Reese's dead-serious eyes and said, "I'll show you I'm a fair man."

"I'm, much obliged," Reese said.

Standing, Gotch found his tailored woolen overcoat and cap with ear flaps. "Upstairs or downstairs?" he asked cheerfully. "Bear's lairs or county fairs?"

"Just a plain hill," Reese said.

"Just like Jack and Jill," Gotch chuckled, "I'm Jack."

Accompanied by the smaller man, Reese went out to the boardwalk, turned left and held his stride.

"You keep your bank swept and dusted every day?" he asked.

"My teller does that every morning before we open the door." Gotch said, hurrying to keep pace alongside the big man.

"Look at that mound there."

"What about it?" the banker sputtered.

"It's a dead dog. Been there a week, and if nobody does anything about it, it'll rot back into the street by spring."

"I'm just one citizen in this town. Gotch said and laughed. "Be careful— walk on a crack, break your grandmother's back!"

"You just told me you own most of it," Reese persisted.

"If all you're going to do is find fault, I'm going back," Gotch retorted, losing his smile.

Before he could turn away, Reese reached out with his maul of a hand, wrapped his fingers around Gotch's left arm and propelled him along without losing his long stride.

"We've got to change," Reese said.

As Reese's steely fingers clamped down on his arm, the banker said, "Of course, it all takes money."

"Not much," Reese said, stepping down from the end of the boardwalk into the littered street and continuing his march to Boot Hill.

"Of course, we could have a community clean-up day, maybe next summer," the banker said, after stumbling over a wheelless perambulator.

As the buildings became fewer and shabbier, vacant lots were piled higher with the town's refuse. Gotch's breath came in quick fuming gusts and his shiny new gaiters slipped in the muck.

The rising trail didn't make it any easier, but Reese held the banker's elbow, lifting him along when he faltered.

The freezing wind blew harder on the open hillside, and Gotch clutched at the collar of his coat, buttoning it tight around his neck as vaporous scuds of frost particles whipped by like whining gray ghosts.

The path leading to the top was slick with ice, and Gotch had trouble with his footing, but Reese held him erect and kept him moving.

Along the way were holes in the earth where dogs or coyotes had dug into graves, and the wooden crosses and headboards that hadn't been tilted by wind and frost, were rubbed down by itching burros.

"Seems like you could afford to put a fence around the place," Reese observed.

"I have no relatives or friends here," Gotch shrugged.

"You don't think there'll come a time....?"

"My future is all taken care of," Gotch said, smiling, as they reached the flattened out crest pocked with clumps of greasewood and cactus.

"The fact of the matter is I intend building a marble mausoleum right here at the very top. You can see my corner stakes." Gotch pointed out the four iron pipes driven into the ground. "I've already purchased a large plot and the plans are drawn for a small Greek temple with a vault made of Italian marble and a bronze casket lined with lead. It is here where I shall lie and look over my land."

Reese chuckled and said, "How you goin' to look through all that lead and marble?"

"I'm glad you see the humor in it," Gotch smiled. "Death is the biggest joke of all."

A reeking stench emanated from a dog dug hole and they moved upwind together.

"And how long in this grubby, little town do you think it would be before someone came up here with an eight pound hammer and started breaking down your Greek temple?"

"We did not win the west with that kind of thinking. Ambition! Ambition is what this country needs!" The rosy checked banker smacked his gloved fist into the palm of the other hand to emphasize the force of his words.

"There's rats livin' here, and rats carry the plague, and the plague doesn't care if you're rich or poor."

"Scare talk," Gotch snorted. "If there are rats, there'll be ambitious cats right behind them."

"I'd say Rose Cameron was plenty ambitious about keepin' her ranch."

"Her husband borrowed money from me. He knew the interest rate and the consequences of not paying it."

"She could have paid it. Those turkeys are out there at the ranch right now, picked, dressed and froze hard as river rocks. She could sell 'em and have money left over."

"Then the joke's on you!" Gotch laughed. "You did all that dirty work for nothing."

"I want you to look around this sorry hill, look at death that's waitin' for us all, and think some on how to make the living better for everybody.'"

"I don't scare. I'm not afraid of death and corruption," Gotch said, turning away.

"Imagine if the people were all helpin' each other whenever some special trouble struck, working together so that every one had a fair chance to live a decent life. Seems to me that ought to be ambition enough."

"Foolishness! It never has happened and never will."

Reese gently turned Gotch around again, looked down at his thin face and said, "You can change this town for the better or you can go it alone to a dug-out grave right here."

"Smile and the world smiles with you," Gotch grinned. "Don't forget Scotsmen have a sense of humor because it's a gift."

"It's Christmas time, man!" Reese said, exasperated.

"Foolishness for fools!" Gotch crowed.

"You're a hopeless case," Reese said, shaking his head and starting down the curving trail that would lead back to main street, leaving the banker behind.

Gotch stared after the big man in the buffalo robe, and thought the wind was rising, the way it seemed to moan louder and louder. Wraiths of scud plunged about him as he stood on his burial plot and proudly looked around to see his great domain.

Yonder would be his Circle C controlling the water, and, off to the west was the Bar D. Easterly was the great tract of sheep land, all falling into his empire before another year passed.

He smiled.

Maybe I'll change the name from Calico to Gotch—Gotchville—Gotchburg—he mused, smiling as if joking with himself—. Calico didn't mean anything, but Gotch will mean the fulfillment of ambition, an example of success for coming generations. Success is never as easy as it looks. Nobody gave all this to me on a silver platter!

Gotchville. Gotch Avenue. Gotch Creek. Gotch Mountains. Gotch Ranch. Gotch Packing Company. Gotch Garden of Memories.

Success will be equated with Gotch; a new word in our lexicon: to Gotch is to win. I gotch the game, you gotch the game, he gotches the game. To the gotcher belongs the spoils!

The grey sleety scud came on thicker and, burying his numb hands in his overcoat pockets, he cheerfully started down the littered and uneven trail.

The path ran by the recent grave of a nameless pauper, and Gotch looked away from the dog-diggings, picking up his pace. He saw a skull lying in the fresh dug earth and wondered why he hadn't seen it on the way up just a few minutes before.

"Foolishness!" he said aloud. "Fool foolishness!"

Hunching his shoulders, he hurried on when an open hand flashed out of the desecrated grave. The hand was dark brown up to the wrist and the rest of the long arm white as pickled pork.

He twisted in terror as the hand grabbed his ankle.

"No!" he screamed as he felt the hand pulling him down.

"No!" he screamed again, just before his head hit a broken tombstone, and all went black.

Chapter Thirteen

*I*n his nose was the smell of raw dirt. Looking up, Max Gotch saw a vaulted marble ceiling supported by eight carved Ionic pillars.

"Let go!" he yelled, but the hand held fast.

In the dim light he felt his shoulder brush against something and moving exploratory fingers to either side, he found he was lying in a box lined with taffeta rotted into tatters. I ordered silk! he thought angrily.

"Where am I?" he called out, his voice echoing back and forth in the miniature Grecian temple.

Hearing a rasping scratching sound against the domed roof, he rubbed his nose and discovered it had disappeared along with the rest of the flesh, and his fingers scraped across the dry bone of his skull.

"Wake up, Max! he told himself. "You're dreaming!"

He tried to force his mind out of the dream and back to reality. Nothing changed. He couldn't move his legs or sit up. His back seemed to be cemented to the bottom of the box.

I'm dead, he thought, and from far away the mournful howl of a great hound sent fearful tremors through the marble tomb.

The scratching sound paused a moment, then started again.

If I'm dead, why have I come back to life, so to speak, he wondered. Maybe it's the day of resurrection, the Great Jubilee when the earth breaks open and we all leap out of our graves, and it's first come, first served!

I can't go out looking like this, he worried. You'd think they'd give us at least a bathrobe or a sheet.

The scratching subsided and an earth tremor shook the tomb. Flakes of paint fell from the ceiling and he glared at the bare patches. I paid for Italian marble, and they gave me painted plaster, he thought.

Another tremor shook the tomb and one of the pillars collapsed into a pile of sawdust.

They cheated me because I couldn't stop payment, he thought bitterly. No respect. No respect at all for what a man stood for.

I suppose it's too late to sue.

He caught a glimpse of movement in the far corner and called out, "Who's there?"

There was no reply and the scratching against the roof commenced again.

In the far corner he saw a pair of luminous blue lights, small but powerful in their intensity.

"Who are you?" he croaked. "Give me a hand."

There was no sound of reply, only the rasping on the roof.

"I say, if you'll help me, I'll see that you get a decent job at the bank," he tried again.

The blue lights disappeared for an instant as if someone had blinked his eyes, and he said, "I'll give you a ten dollars if you'll help me out."

He thought he heard a low chuckling sound and he said sharply, "It's not funny. I can't move."

"You will never move again," a dry voice chortled, "not until you have killed ten rats."

He couldn't believe his ears. Who was whispering? Who had a giggle like that?

"Speak up," Gotch commanded. "Name yourself."

"I am the auditor," the whisperer said, jovially. "I check the books. Are your accounts in order?"

"Well, this is awfully short notice!" Max Gotch protested. "I wonder if we couldn't just have a meeting of the minds. I expect to see you rewarded for your courtesy, of course. One hand washes the other, as we say...." Gotch tried to chuckle, but his jaws rattled like a dried gourd.

"The last man who offered me a bribe is now working as a rat skinner."

"And where might that be?" Gotch asked nervously.

"Down in the shadowed Valley of the Rats," the voice whispered playfully. "Think about that before you open your ledgers for audit."

"And what do naughty bankers do in the Valley of the Rats?" Gotch stammered. "I mean they should get some credit for public service...."

"Most bankers work as house cleaners in the rat village," the whisperer replied, laughing. "If they have bribed public officials and robbed their depositors, then they are confined to the rats' quarters as well."

"You mean they have to live with the rats?" Gotch exclaimed.

"As they lived, so shall they die. A funny eternity for the money fraternity," replied the merry auditor. "Are you ready?"

"Suppose a banker happened to die the day before Christmas? Shouldn't you give him some bonus, a little extra favor?" Gotch stammered fearfully.

"He gets what he gave," laughter echoed through the earth smelling chamber. "All set for the summing up?"

"I'm not feeling well," the banker complained. "Maybe you could come back tomorrow?"

"No."

"What's the scratching on the roof?" Gotch asked, stalling for time.

"Rats," came the jolly whisper. "They're coming for you."

"Me!" cried out Max Gotch. "I'm a respectable business-man!"

Dust fell away from the scaly ceiling and the scratching noise grew louder. Far away the great hound dog bayed in misery.

"You get what you gave...." The dry whisper merrily floated through the musty air.

Gotch tried to shrink aside, screaming, "No! No!" as a hole in the vaulted ceiling opened and two red eyes peered into the tomb.

"No! No! No!" he screamed as the ceiling opened wider and half a dozen squealing rats came falling toward his white, gasping face....

"Hold still," came a harsh voice, and Gotch felt two powerful hands lock down on his shoulders. "Hold still or you'll break it again."

Gotch opened his eyes and saw the big man in black bending over him, pinning him to the table.

"I'm nearly finished," another voice said. "Good thing you knocked yourself out, Mr. Gotch, you might have felt some pain."

Gotch looked down at the end of the table and saw Doctor Snarph wrapping a splint on his right ankle.

"What happened?" he groaned.

"I waited for you to come back into town, then I went back up and found you lying with your head next to a chunk of tombstone, your foot in a hole. Broke your ankle," Reese said quietly, releasing his hold.

"He carried you over his shoulder to my office," the doctor added. "Good thing, too. If nobody'd gone looking for you, you'd have froze to death up there by now."

Touching his fingers to the bandaged lump on the side of his head, Gotch murmured, "Thank you, Mr. Reese."

"I'll rent you a pair of crutches," Doctor Snarph said.

"I keep remembering... the hand..." Gotch murmured worriedly, "and an... auditor that giggled... Oh... the grinning rats! Oh, now I remember!"

"Maybe I better give you a dose of laudanum to steady your nerves," the Doctor said, staring at the white faced banker. "You're delirious from the concussion."

"I'm all right!" Gotch said quickly. "It's just I remember... something...."

Carrying his sacked bundle, Joel Reese strode down the street toward the gulch crossing.

In the bitter cold, his breath looked like smoke, and ice crystals formed on his thick, untrimmed mustache.

Going into Ira's Bar 'n Grill, he sat at the counter and placed the bundle on the floor.

Ira looked out from the kitchen and called, "Mornin', stranger. You almost missed breakfast. Merry Christmas!"

"Good morning," Joel replied. "I've lost track of the time...."

"Tomorrow's Christmas Day," Ira laughed, ladling flapjack batter onto the griddle.

"I'm looking for Mrs. Cameron," Joel said.

"Right here," Rose said grimly, coming out of the kitchen.

"Good morning, ma'am," Reese said. "I don't aim to bother you, but there's some settlin' up to do before I ride on."

Rose poured him a cup of coffee, and Ira yelled through the window, "Flapjacks on the rise."

"Settling up?" she muttered grimly. "I don't owe you anything."

"How's the boy?" Reese asked.

"The fever goes up and it goes down, but it doesn't go away," Rose said, forgetting her animosity. "It seems like he can't get up spunk enough to fight it. "

"Leadbellies!" Ira called, putting the chipped plate stacked with flapjacks on the shelf.

Rose placed it in front of Reese, added the butter dish and sorghum jar, and Reese ate like a hungry wolf.

"I'd like to look at him, if you don't mind," Reese said sopping up the last of the buttery molasses. "I brought him a little Christmas present."

"I don't see any harm in it," Rose said, eyeing the big man suspiciously.

Rose led him down the hall to the bedroom where Lena dozed in the chair and Tommy lay with his bare arms outside the covers, his face pale and his breath rasping out in short gusts.

Reese put the sacked bundle on the bureau and sat on the bed alongside the boy, studying his face, touching his brow with the back of his calloused fingers.

Shaking his head silently, he took Tommy's left hand and turned the wrist over, examining it closely, then he repeated the examination on the right arm, saying nothing as Rose watched.

Beckoning to her, he went out into the hall and asked quietly, "Those little marks on the inside of his right forearm....?"

"Those?" Rose frowned as she remembered. "It was sometime last week. I left him in the buckboard in the alley behind the Mercantile. He got to fooling around in the trash and found a rat's nest with little ones in it. I guess he got a surprise when he reached in and mama rat nipped him."

"It figures," Reese said heavily. "We had an epidemic at Fort Donelson."

"You mean that little bite—"

"The men lingered, feverish, but the fever'd never break."

"But that was back east," Rose said.

"It goes where the rats go. Maybe it'd cheer him up some if you showed him that present when he wakes up," Joel said.

"Maybe you aren't all bad," Rose said looking at him straight forwardly. "Maybe you had to burn up the turkey pen just to keep from freezing."

"That house had as much ice on the inside as it did on the outside," Joel nodded.

"Deep down, I knew you couldn't save my turkeys," Rose confessed. "Nobody could in this storm."

"Ma'am when I saw they were about to freeze, I killed 'em quick so they'd bleed clean. Then I picked and dressed 'em out. All but the three biggest ones."

"How could you do that?" Rose asked in surprise. "Why, it would take all night!"

"It kept me warm," Reese nodded.

"I suppose they're spoiled by now, though." Rose shook her head.

"Not likely. They're frozen hard down in your root cellar."

Rose heard Tommy groan, and hurried back into the bedroom.

Going out the front door, Reese made his way back across the gulch, wondering if he could ever leave this country with a clear conscience. Somehow every time he tried to help out, he just dug himself in deeper.

He paid Elroy Morrison a dollar to release Rose Cameron's team, and after harnessing them to the buckboard, he drove out of town at a fast trot.

The ranch looked not only deserted, but abandoned. The icy wind moaned around the corners of the grey buildings, and a shutter flapped loosely on the barn.

He thought he heard voices and the distant bawl of cattle to the north, but the ranch belonged to Gotch now, and Reese was finished with it.

He halted the buckboard near the root cellar and hauled out the crates of frozen turkeys. Once loaded in the back of the buckboard, he lashed a tarp over the top to keep them clean and cold.

As he was about to climb up to the buckboard seat, Colonel Wayne Damker, on a big winter shaggy roan rode into the yard.

Seeing Reese, he pulled up and looked at him bleakly as if daring him to start a ruckus.

"Howdy," Reese said.

"You'll find some Circle C cattle up yonder," Damker said, nudging his roan forward. "Tell the truth, they strayed over about six months ago and I figured to turn 'em back over here, but old Gotch got wind of it and kind of hinted he'd give me an extension on my note if I just kept 'em on my grass awhile."

"You're some late, Damker. The widow woman went broke and sold out to the banker," Reese said levelly. "He's your new neighbor, and if I was you, I'd feel like a puppy dog bunkin' next to an alligator."

"I didn't know she was that bad off..." Damker said grimly. "Maybe if we talked to Gotch, he'd let up some."

"I talked to him," Reese shook his head, and climbed up into the seat. "He don't listen."

Downcast and silent, Colonel Damker turned his roan and rode west toward the Bar D.

Driving the buckboard out the iron gate, he met Fortunato Fajardo and his herder, both mounted on ribby pinto ponies.

"Afternoon'," Reese said, eyeing Fortunato.

"Buenos tardes," Fortunato said. "I see Bar D putting Cameron's cattle back on their range. I think maybe I better put back the mares a man sold me."

"Fast talkin' jasper?"

"That's the man. He was riding a big old stud branded Circle C. The others were not branded,. He was in a hurry, and I bought them all for fifty dollars. He cursed me, but he took my money. Later I began thinking those mares might be from here."

"Somethin' sort of jogged your memory?" Reese asked, looking Fortunato straight in the eye.

"My wife remembered..." Fortunato nodded humbly. "Tomorrow's Christmas."

"The lady went out of business first thing this mornin', but I reckon she'd appreciate the horses anyway," Reese said, slapping the reins, setting the team back toward town.

With evening coming on, the downhill grade and almost five hundred pounds of turkeys in the back pushed the team along at a fast trot.

Driving the buckboard directly into the shadowed livery barn, Reese found Elroy Morrison leaning on a pitchfork, contemplating a hill of manure.

"I need a cold place where there's no dogs or cats." Reese said jerking his thumb at his lashed down cargo.

"Park it over there in the northwest stall. It's the coldest, and I don't let any stray animals in here, including rats."

"Fine." Reese nodded, unhitching the team. "It won't be for long."

"Whatcha got in there?" Morrison asked, his eyes on the bulging tarp.

"Turkeys. Ready to roast, Merry Christmas to you," Reese said.

In the twilight he strode off toward the gulch, then, suddenly aware that something was changed, he stopped to stare at a bonfire burning in the middle of the town square attended by people coming and going.

Almost every man in town was carrying something: split boxes, broken— spoked wagon wheels, barrel staves, packing crates, rags, discarded harnesses, all the varied trash in Calico, to the growing fire.

"What's goin' on?" Reese asked an old man in a many-patched overcoat, pushing a torn, hay filled mattress in a wheelbarrow toward the fire.

"Rats," the old timer hollered. "Mayor Gotch is payin' men ten dollars a day to clean out the rats and run 'em out of town."

"Good money," Reese said.

"I reckon I can make Christmas with it," the old man grinned, shoving the iron wheelbarrow forward.

In the pale winter light, Reese saw men with rakes and pitchforks cleaning out under the boardwalks, and grey rats, big and small, scuttling down the street, heading for the open spaces.

Another man with a team of horses pulling a Fresno, was scraping the manure off the street clear down to new dirt.

Passing by the fire, Reese saw Max Gotch on crutches, a smile on his cheery face, and heard him yelling, "Go get 'em, boys! Run them devils out!"

Wondering what had made the banker so suddenly dedicated to cleaning up the town, Reese saw that some of the men were tossing unburnable trash, bottles, an old tin oven, broken chamber pots, ruined queen's ware, powder cans, holed washtubs, rusted out stovepipe, and half a whiskey still, onto a big dray being pulled along slowly by four mules.

The man means business, Reese thought as he crossed the gulch and came to Ira's Bar 'n Grill dimly lighted inside by a coal oil lamp.

Ira sat at the counter, his shoulders bowed over a cup of coffee.

"How's the boy?" Reese asked, closing the door.

Ira didn't look up, but continued staring morosely at the thick mug of coffee.

In the hallway, Reese looked inside the lamp-lighted bedroom. Four women held vigil over the fever-exhausted boy whose labored breathing came raggedly and so slowly it seemed each breath would be his last.

"How—"

Rose looked at him, her eyes wet and haggard, shook her head, and whispered, "It's worse."

"Well, dang it!" Reese growled angrily, "we're not goin' to quit on him!"

"Doc Snarph is out of town," a wizened lady next to the bed said with a questioning look on her wrinkled face. "You a medico?"

"No, ma'am," Reese said, "but I know a little about fevers."

As Reese looked down at the boy, Rose said, "Nellie Damker, Anaberta Fajardo, Lena McCoy, this is Joel Reese. He's been helpin' me."

"Pleased to meet you ladies," Reese said, adding "Does anyone know for sure what's wrong?"

"He can't swallow nothing," Anaberta said softly.

"And the fever just keeps on burnin' him up," Lena said.

"His lungs are filling up like it's pneumonia," Nellie offered sadly. "I'm sure sorry, Rose."

"He's got to sweat," Reese said decisively. "If you ladies will fetch me a basin, some flour sacks and a couple teakettles of boiling hot water right away...."

"What...?" Nellie frowned.

"Hurry it up!" Reese snapped, already rolling up his sleeves.

As the women hurried out the door, he asked Rose, "Did he see his present?"

"No, we were so busy," Lena said, shaking her head. "We never got around to it."

Reese went to the bureau, took the small new saddle from the gunny sack, and hung it over the headboard of the bed.

"It's Christmas Eve, Tommy," he said heavily. "Don't let me down."

In a minute the ladies returned with the basin, a steaming teakettle, and a stack of clean flour sacks, and Rose moved out of the way.

"War teaches strange lessons," Joel said, dunking a sack into the scalding hot water, and pulling the covers away from Tommy's bare chest. "Teaches survival... teaches caring... teaches last resorts...."

"De mangas o de faldas...." Anaberta said worriedly. "One way or another."

Joel wrung the excess water from the cloth and laid it steaming on the thin chest. He lifted the boy's arms in an arc over his head to the pillow, then brought them back down again, trying to increase Tommy's blood circulation.

"There you go, trooper," Reese said with mock gruffness., "Warm you up some."

"That's awful hot," Nellie worried.

"I hope you know what you're doing," Lena frowned.

"It's now or never," Joel said stubbornly. "Help me out, Tom."

In a moment, he followed the first cloth with a second and pumped the arms up and down again and again until the boy stirred uncomfortably.

"You're scaldin' him," Rose Cameron said nervously.

"Keep that water comin' hotter'n Hades," Reese retorted, replacing the second cloth with a third, and pumping the boy's arms. "We got to sweat the poison out of him."

Anaberta brought in a full teakettle and replaced the empty one.

"Come on, Tom," Reese said, "Ride with me."

The boy's chest was turning red from the heat and he commenced a coughing spell that seemed to tear his lungs to pieces, but the big man in black, unrelenting, continued with hot steaming towels and pumping the arms, until Rose cried out, "You're just boilin' him alive!"

The sharp sound of her voice seemed to penetrate Tommy's mind. He opened his eyes and stared up at the saddle hanging over his head.

"Merry Christmas, Tom," Reese said, applying another steaming towel. "Pretty soon you're goin' to be settin' that saddle."

The boy said nothing. His eyes closed, his slow breath rattled from his congested lungs as if it were his last.

"Oh Mother of God!" Lena whimpered in terror, and Anaberta silently made the sign of the cross.

"He seen it," Reese said, changing the hot towel again.

The boy's face seemed to be aflame with fever, his cheeks flushed scarlet, his forehead red as rubies. Fearfully Rose leaned over and touched his face.

"Sweat...!"

Reese saw the faint sheen of moisture on the boy's forehead, gradually increasing to a viscous film breaking into yellowish beads, and the beads forming into rivulets flowing off his face.

"You'll do, Tommy. You'll do," Reese said gruffly.

"Oh, thank thee, blessed Providence," Rose Cameron murmured softly, laying her head on Tommy's shoulder.

Tears ran down Anaberta's plump face, and Nellie put her arm around her shoulder and said huskily, "What the hell you bawlin' about, girl?"

"I'm so happy!" Anaberta choked out, weeping.

"It's broke! The fever's broke!" Lena called down the hall to Ira and a group of neighbors who had come in to wait out Tommy's fate together.

"Poison's just awashin' out of him!"

Tommy opened his eyes again, looked up at the saddle and whispered, "The saddle?"

"Handmade to your order and ready for ridin', cowboy." Reese said, bringing the comforters up over Tommy's chest and wiping the flowing sweat from his face.

"Oh! No!" Rose groaned in pain, leaning over and putting her hands to her back.

Chapter Fourteen

*D*awn came clear and crisp, flooding on a rosy glow from the far eastern horizon, the radiant light touching each building and person and the frost whitened ground, and when the great orange sun lifted up from the saw-toothed Calicos, the cold wind gradually shifted to the south.

Early risers looked up and down Calico's frosty streets with wonder. Not a stray crate nor mound of horse manure remained, not an empty bottle nor abandoned cart cluttered the way.

"Clean as a whistle," George Veiten called over to Dill Rafferty, and smiled. "Merry Christmas to you!"

"Same to you, George," Rafferty called back cheerily. "Ain't it a wonder though what a little clean-up will do! I'm thinkin' of paintin' the Calico Queen to keep up with the times."

"Paint's dear," Veiten said cautiously. "Still, you know, the town looks kind of drab now that the rest of it's so tidy."

Marshal Wolford strolled down the middle of the street and wished both men a Merry Christmas.

"Sure looks nice, don't it?" Rafferty said.

"It's goin' to stay that way, too," Marshal Wolford said. "First one that throws his trash out in the street is goin' to answer to me."

"Ha!" Veiten laughed. "Now we goin' to make you the town rat trapper!"

"Ain't no rats left," the Marshal said. "They fogged out of town headin' west in a herd, and first one tries to come back I'm goin' to punch a hole right between his eyes."

"Good mornin' gents," Ophelia Masson greeted them cheerfully, "Merry Christmas to you all."

The men replied in kind, and George Veiten called out, "Need a hand with that broom?"

"Not likely, thanks," she replied. "I saw you fellers out sweepin' the boardwalk, and figured I better do my share."

"We're talkin' about paintin'," Dill Rafferty called over.

"Wouldn't that be nice," Ophelia Masson agreed. "I'd like the hotel to be white with blue trim."

"Merry Christmas everyone!" called out Max Gotch, stumping down the boardwalk on crutches. "Are we having a town meeting on this grand day?"

"We're goin' to paint the whole town!" Dill Rafferty responded proudly.

"Red?" Gotch asked solemnly, and in the puzzled quiet that followed, suddenly burst out laughing. "What I mean let's have some fun doing it!"

The others, infected by the banker's good humor, grinned and Dill Rafferty said they'd paint the bank gold if Gotch would pay for the paint.

"No," Gotch smiled, "the red brick will do, but next year on the first of December, I'll see that there's a big Christmas tree right in the center of the square."

Leaving the group to their discussion, Max Gotch swung along on his crutches, his peppermint stick muffler ruffling over his grey shoulder cape, his little goat-roper hat set at a jaunty angle, his head high, greeting everyone he met with a hearty, "Merry Christmas!"

Crossing the gulch, he pegged up the slope to Ira's and without pausing, went inside where a group of poorly dressed men and women huddled over coffee mugs at the counter.

In the shadowed room he made out a Paiute Indian, a couple of Mexican charcoal burners, buckskin clad trappers, Aunt Sally Mae and old Ed, then the big cowboy dressed in black, Joel Reese, and near him, close to the stove, lay the Cameron boy on a pallet, covered with a blanket.

Behind the counter, pegleg Ira Armsbury, heavy-shouldered and heavy-faced, was pouring coffee from a huge enamel ware pot.

"Merry Christmas everyone!" Gotch called out, trying to bring some cheer to the dismal group. "The wind's changing."

He received only a mumbled response and a nodding of heads.

From somewhere in the back of the building he heard a woman groan in pain, and sensing this was connected to the worry in the room, Gotch crutched over to the counter and quietly asked Ira, "What is it?"

"Mrs. Cameron," Ira muttered. "She went into labor about midnight. She's havin' an awful hard time of it."

"She was just plain worn out to begin with," Aunt Sally Mae said, nodding.

"Do you want me to call Doctor Snarph?" Max Gotch asked, easing himself down onto the end stool. "Just say the word."

"Doc's out of town." Ira shook his head, adding, "but she's got plenty of help."

"And you, Tommy, how are you this grand Christmas morning?" Gotch smiled down at the pinched face and big eyes.

"Just fine, sir," Tommy replied in a small voice.

"Don't you worry about your mother, son," Gotch said. "She's as good and strong as they come."

"Yes, sir," Tommy nodded. "See my saddle?"

Gotch picked up the small saddle next to the boy, looked it over from stirrup taps to roping horn, lastly reading the silver plate on the cantle.

"Boy, that's a dandy! You'll get a lot of good use out of that...."

"I guess not," the boy murmured.

"Nonsense," the banker said, misunderstanding, "you'll be riding like the wind in no time."

"Where?" Tommy asked, and the room seemed to go quiet and hold its breath.

"I'm going to talk to your mother about that, Tommy," Max Gotch smiled. "But first, I'd like to speak to you—" he added, turning to face the man in black.

"I'm here. Been here all night," Reese said, his voice tired and spiritless from the long hours of vigil.

"And you haven't accomplished anything except bog yourself down," the banker grinned, and got up on the crutches again. "Come along, Mr. Reese, we've got real things to do."

"I'm stayin' here in case I'm needed," Reese said.

"You can do nothing to change nature, young man. But I did hear you have a load of frozen turkeys. We can do something about that."

Reese rose slowly and asked, "What about those turkeys?"

"I wish to buy them all. I want every family in Calico to have a turkey dinner, and I want you to drive me around town so that no one is missed. Fair enough?"

"Fair enough," Reese said, a slow smile coming to his glum features. "Let's go."

"Just a minute," Gotch said and turned to Ira again. "Ira, there'll be some of those birds left over and everyone in town without a family can have Christmas dinner here, if that suits you."

"Spread the word, I'll fire up the oven." Ira's big, lop-sided face split into a wide grin.

As they went out the door, Gotch called, "We'll be back with bells on and whistles blowing!"

Outside the south wind had lost its icy bite and dropped to a gentle breeze, bringing an end to the killing cold, and Joel Reese slowed to the banker's crutching pace. The warming fresh air felt good in his lungs and there seemed a new buoyance in the people as if spring had arrived early.

"Merry Christmas," Gotch greeted Elroy Morrison.

"I'm goin" to paint the whole shebang bright yellow with white trim. Lighten it up around here," Morrison said, as if he'd been waiting to get it off his chest. "How can I help you?"

"We'll want the buckboard and team," Reese said.

"Let me hitch 'em up." Elroy hurried into the barn, emerging minutes later leading the team and buckboard out the double doors.

"There you are, gents, Merry Christmas!" Elroy Morrison smiled as Reese undid the lashing over the tarp, and knocked his fist against one of the sacks.

"Thawing out," he said to the banker, helping him up into the buckboard's seat.

"That's fine. We want them ready for the oven," Gotch said cheerfully. "Let's start over on the northwest with Mrs. Feldcamp. She's got a flock of little ones."

Reese drove the team through the clean vacant lots and bare land to an adobe hut with a sod roof and when a lean, lank woman with hollow eyes came out, followed by a brood of small children in patched hand-me-downs, Gotch reached back for a frozen turkey in a flour sack and added two silver dollars to buy a few trimmings.

"Many thanks to you, mister, many thanks!" she called out in numb surprise as they pulled away.

With Reese driving from house to house, Gotch presented a turkey and two silver dollars to each family and a rousing 'Merry Christmas', until they had covered all of Calico.

Reese drove back toward Ira's place, and Gotch counted the remaining turkeys and said, "Five. You think that's enough for everyone, Joel?"

"I think that's enough, Max," Reese smiled.

They entered the cafe, with Reese carrying the sacked turkeys back into the kitchen while Gotch took the end stool where he could stretch out his splinted ankle.

Slipping a twenty dollar gold piece across the counter, Gotch whispered in Ira's ear, "Maybe you could send an order over to the Mercantile for some yams and pickles and candy, whatever, and maybe a couple bottles of Spanish brandy?"

"Right away, Mr. Gotch," Ira smiled.

"Hey, Ira, my name's Max," Gotch grinned. "Merry Christmas!"

Ira smiled, shook his head, and tried it out. "Max...
Max... all right, Max. Merry Christmas!"

From the bedroom once again came the slow groan of a
woman in difficult labor biting her lips.

Rose Cameron lay on the bed, her hands grasping the
twisted sheet strung from the headboard posts, her head
propped on pillows, her pale face wet with sweat as the
tremor passed.

Gathered around her were Nellie, Anaberta, and Lena,
their varied faces solemn and concerned in the pale light.

"He's a stubborn little cuss," Rose groaned, "and I'm so
tired...."

Lena bowed over the bed, put her small hand on Rose's
abdomen and said, "Steady on Rose, slow but sure."

"He's not crooked or anything, is he?" Rose asked worriedly.

"I figure he's just taking his time because you're so run
down," Nellie said, shaking her head. "Now bear down hard."

"Is always different." Anaberta said, "and never easy."

The contraction came a minute later and once again
Rose's face contorted with pain and effort. When it dwindled
away, she closed her eyes and tried to hoard her strength. She
felt she'd never been so tired in her whole life.

"On! I'm worn out..." Rose gasped. "I can't do it...."

"It's goin' to get harder, Rose...." Lena's voice was close
to pleading.

"Damn it, Rose, you've just got to hold up to it." Nellie
snapped.

"You can do it, Rose," Anaberta murmured, "We're with
you."

"I don't know,... I'm so weary, I'm like to die...."

To make the stuffing, Ira commenced tearing up stale loaves of sourdough bread he'd been saving for pudding.

"I got to keep busy, Max," he said. "Screamin' women make me nervous."

"We have to think on the bright side, Ira," Max Gotch said. "Won't be long before there's a new important person in the world."

"I never thought I'd hear you talk like that," Reese said softly.

"Credit yourself, Joel. I got to thinking about what you said up there on Boot Hill, and... after awhile... I made up my mind you were right."

Young Martin Veiten parked a cart full of groceries by the front door and carried in a bag of yams under one arm and a bag of onions in the other.

"Here's your order and some extra Dad put in," the youth said, setting down the bags on the kitchen counter and going out for more.

"Like the man said, Joel," Max Gotch grinned, "the coat and pants do all the work, but the vest gets the gravy."

"And here's the brandy," young Veiten said, putting two bottles of brandy on the counter in front of the banker, "and Papa threw in some wine for the ladies. Merry Christmas, everyone!"

The room was now crowded with anxious men and women worrying about Rose and her painful struggle to bring forth new life, new hope, new faith in man's goodness.

As shadows lengthened, the room grew so dark and gloomy, Max Gotch whispered to Ira, "Got any candles?"

"Sure. I always keep some around," Ira muttered worriedly.

"Let's light 'em all! Brighten the corners.... We're going to have us a celebration soon!" Gotch crowed cheerfully. "And let's open the brandy too!"

Once again Max Gotch's enthusiasm rallied the group's spirits. After the candles were lighted, Ira opened a bottle of brandy and a bottle of wine, poured into chipped cups, odd glasses, and small jars, and passed them around.

Max Gotch got to his feet, lifted his cup and said, "You know folks, a Scotsman can drink any given amount...." when he heard Rose cry out once.... twice.... three times....

The shocked stillness in the candle lighted room was shattered by a final long shriek that fell away to a thread, followed by a grand squall of protest.

"It's a girl!" Lena called out from the hallway. "We got us a fine little girl!"

After a moment of stunned silence, they all rose to their feet, joy radiating from each person's face as Max Gotch croaked, "A toast to the miracle, the precious miracle of life!"

"The miracle!"

As the group drank and settled down into a relieved quietude, Ira boomed out, "What's the matter, everybody dried up all of a sudden?"

"Maybe I could say something serious, kind of an old poem my mother taught me at Christmas," Max Gotch said hesitantly.

"Go ahead, Max," Ira said. "I reckon it won't hurt us none."

Gotch closed his eyes, remembering:

"Today all hatred dies
And tenderness is reborn.
The most misplaced heart
Now knows that someone cares.
Heaven is no longer alone.
Earth is no longer in darkness."

"Amen to that," old Ed said shakily.

Joel Reese leaned over the counter, hoisted Tommy to his shoulder and lifted his glass. "Let's toast Tom and the family...."

"Don't forget the animals," Tommy piped, a smile lighting his face. "The horses—"

"And cattle!" Fortunato Fajardo exclaimed.

"And sheep," Colonel Wayne Damker roared right back.

As the cafe filled with the aroma of roasting turkey and pumpkin pies, the motley group, including Shorty and Ignacio, chattered with relaxed conviviality and didn't stop when Lena, her freckled face scrubbed and red hair combed, tapped Max Gotch, Joel Reese, Wayne Damker, Fortunato Fajardo, and pegleg Ira on their shoulders and jerked her head toward the hall.

Reese, carrying Tommy, moved along with the group to the lamplit bedroom where Rose lay, her head supported by several pillows. Standing to her right, Nellie eyed the gathering, and to her left, Anaberta crouched over the bed, smoothing Rose's hair back.

Lena sat quietly in a chair beside her. Back in the shadows, Ophelia and Elijah Masson stood like protective sentinels, a sense of new pride in their posture.

Rose held a red-faced, black-haired baby wrapped in the pink and blue lambs wool blanket to her breast.

"Isn't she nice, Tommy?" Rose murmured. "She's ours, and we're her's."

"Gosh... she's pitiful small...." Tommy breathed in wonder.

"Ma'am... Rose...." Max Gotch stepped forward, stammering, "Congratulations. Also, I want to give you a Christmas present."

"You don't owe me nothing, Mr. Gotch," Rose said tiredly.

"Please it's a gift, Rose," he said anxiously, putting a document at her side. "I don't want that blamed ranch."

With damp eyes, Rose murmured, "About the only way to thank you is for us to make somethin' good out of the Circle C and help out the rest of the valley."

"Rose, don't forget la Candelaria," Anaberta whispered, "and El Dia de Amistad."

"Anaberta wants us to celebrate all the special holidays," Rose said, nodding. "Candlemas is coming up next, and right after that comes the Dia de Amistad."

"What's so special about Candlemas?" Max Gotch asked.

"It's the day to honor Godparents," Rose said, "and Ophelia and Elijah are going to stand up for this baby."

"Is good, many fiestas," Anaberta said strongly. "Everybody happy."

"And Dia de Amistad?" Reese asked.

"The day of friendship, Joel," Rose said, looking into his eyes, "we call it Valentine's Day."

"These gents found most of your missing horses and cattle off in the coulees somewhere," suddenly red faced, Reese stammered in confusion. "You've got somethin' to start with."

Damker and Fajardo nodded, shifted their boots nervously, and looked down at their hats in their hands.

"Thank you both for caring about us," Rose said. "The old stud in the bunch?"

"No, ma'am, he's long gone with your hired hand," Reese said.

"Your black is about half Morgan, isn't he?" Rose looked directly at him, her eyes honest and steadfast.

"Yes, ma'am," Reese replied awkwardly, "but I figure to drift on...."

"She can't run a horse ranch without a stud," Max Gotch said, reprovingly.

"You sound right ungrateful, Mister," Nellie said sharply.

"Likely she saved your life givin' you shelter in the storm," Colonel Damker said, backing up his wife.

"Mas vale atole con rises, que chocolate con lagrimas," Anaberta intoned solemnly, her dark eyes shining.

"She's saying 'it's better to drink atole with laughter, than chocolate with tears'," Fortunato said, grinning.

"If it'll help out some, I reckon I could stay on awhile," Reese stammered weakly.

"Could you?" Rose murmured.

"I'd need somebody to side me workin' all them colts," Reese nodded, looking over at Tommy.

"I'm ready," Tommy piped up.

"That sounds sensible," Rose said, a trace of a smile playing over her lamplit face.

Ira cleared his throat and backed out of the room, and after Lena, Gotch, the Damkers, the Massons, and the Fajardos followed, Reese said, "You foxed me, Rose."

"Yes, Joel," Rose murmured. "Do you mind?"

"I reckon I'm overdue for a change," Reese said, and Tommy riding his shoulder, whispered excitedly, "Listen!"

From the front room came the swelling chorus of enthusiastic if somewhat rusty voices:

"Should auld acquaintance be forgot
And never brought to mind?
Should auld acquaintance be forgot
And days of auld lang syne?"

In the festive front room, Lena impetuously took Anaberta's hand in her right hand and Nellie's hand in her left. Nellie grinned and grabbed the hand of Ophelia Masson who with a laugh, in turn seized Ira's tattooed mitt, and so it went around and around as they sang. When, hand in hand, the ring of celebrants came to the chorus, Lena cried out, "Everybody! Loud and clear!"

While in the bedroom, Rose, Joel and Tommy listened in amazement as the chorus filled the whole barn.

"For auld lang syne, my dear,
For auld lang syne,
We'll take a cup of kindness yet
For days of auld lang syne...!"

"They're all together!" Tommy cried out, laughing.

"And listen to that sweet harmony," Rose said softly, closing her eyes.

Outside a multitude of downy flakes of snow floated on the gentle south breeze, a host of chaste glosses hovering and drifting in the magically congested atmosphere, changing the sky from grey rags to clouds of cotton lint sifting slowly down to rest on the valley and the hills like a white comforter of plenitude and peace.